MY MOTHER'S GHOST

MY MOTHER'S GHOST
Margaret Buffie

KIDS CAN PRESS LTD.
TORONTO

Kids Can Press Ltd. acknowledges with appreciation the assistance of the Canada Council and the Ontario Arts Council in the production of this book.

Canadian Cataloguing in Publication Data
Buffie, Margaret.
My mother's ghost

ISBN 1-55074-114-4 (bound). - ISBN 1-55074-091-1 (pbk.)

I. Title.

PS8553.U453M8 1992   jC813'.54   C92-093409-9
PZ7.B84My 1992

Kids Can Press Ltd.
585 1/2 Bloor Street West
Toronto, Ontario, Canada
M6G 1K5

Edited by Charis Wahl
Cover design by N. R. Jackson
Interior design by Esperança Melo

Printed and bound in Canada

92 0 9 8 7 6 5 4 3 2 1

This book is dedicated to the memory of my mother,
Evelyn Elizabeth Leach, 1916-1989

CHAPTER 1

"COME ON, JESS. LET'S GET TO WORK, EH?"

I didn't answer. I'd had enough of my father for one day. And it was only six a.m. He'd just listed every detail he had planned for the day while spraying toast crumbs and swilling coffee. Now, he stood up, rubbing his hands together.

"What a day, eh, Jess? Our first group of paying guests. Everything has to be perfect. I don't want one towel or bar of soap missing from a guest cabin."

"I told you, it's all ready," I snapped. "Winny's done this a million times before, remember?"

"Just because she's worked here for thirty years doesn't mean she's always done a good job, does it? After all, her last boss sold out." He grabbed his hat off the wall hook.

"Yeah, right, Dad. Her last boss, *Mrs.* Parks, is in an old-age home. Silly reason to sell out."

But he wasn't listening. "We've got fifteen horses and all those sets of tack to sort out. I expect you to help me first thing this morning."

I picked up his mug and plate. "I'll be right there. I'll just stick these in the sink and put away the cereal and stuff."

"Two minutes. No more."

The screen door clacked shut. He trotted towards the corrals, the rolling fog gathering him in. I put the cup and plate in the sink and gripped the edge of the counter. I still couldn't believe we were living in this dump in the foothills of Alberta. What had he been thinking of, buying a broken-down guest ranch? He didn't know a thing about running a business like this.

He'd had other stupid ideas before, like buying a pizza parlour, but Mom had persuaded him to think about it— until the idea wore off. After pizza, it was video and health-food stores, and even a market garden, but she'd known how to handle him then. Of course, that was before the world tipped over on us.

Was it only two months ago Dad announced he'd had enough of working behind a desk? That's when he quit the R.C.M.P. and bought Willow Creek Ranch, a thousand miles away from home. Mom hadn't even put up a fight—she was in pretty bad shape by then—and I could complain all I wanted, but it didn't change anything. Mom had ignored the movers packing around her and had let Dad tuck her into the back seat of the car. She didn't look up once while we drove down our tree-lined street, away from Winnipeg... Winnipeg and my little brother, Scotty.

Dad's shrill whistle cut through the haze-filled air. Most of the horses would come running at the sound, but others would stay in the far pasture, cropping sweet grass. Someone would have to saddle up and get the laggards. Well, he could find them himself. I was not getting on another horse.

Behind me, one of the ancient kitchen chairs creaked. When I looked over my shoulder, she was putting the milk carton on the table. Resting her arms on either side of her bowl, she stared into the cereal, thumbs tucked inside tight fists. I'd been hoping to avoid her.

"Mom?"

She gazed around vaguely. When she found me, she managed a half smile and looked back down at her cereal. I tried to be as patient as I could, but sometimes all I felt was a hot prickly irritation at her uncombed hair and grubby terry bathrobe.

"You okay?" I asked, trying not to sound sharp.

"I'm just fine." She pushed back the bowl. Milk slopped onto the table. "I'm just not hungry. I ate too much last night, I guess."

It wasn't true, but arguing, I'd learned, only changed the dead look in her eyes to one of wary confusion. The point about last night was that we'd sat around the huge barbecue pit with Winny and her husband, Percy Eldridge, while Dad made a big production of cooking some of the huge steaks he'd bought for the weekend guests. Mom had dropped hers bit by bit into her napkin. Later, when Dad went with Percy to do some work out in the paddocks, she threw the full napkin onto the smouldering coals.

She hardly ate anything any more. But did my father notice? Not him. He was like a little kid before Christmas — over-excited and given to tantrums. Nothing was going to interfere with his first mountain trek.

He refused to see that Mom had been getting worse since we got here — paler, thinner— less substantial. I was scared she'd go completely inside herself. Soon it might be too late to help her. I'd tried everything I could think of, but I knew I wouldn't be able to make things turn out right for her. And that scared me a lot. I guess that's why I got so irritated — why couldn't she force herself to do things? All she ever did was sleep or lie on her bed, staring at the ceiling. When she was vertical, she drifted through the old ranch house like a ghost — silently mourning Scotty.

Of course, no one asked me how *I* was doing. I thought moving away would maybe take the ache out of my gut, this hollow ache that never went away — but it didn't. It couldn't be possible that Scotty was dead. Things like that happened to other people. How could he be gone, just like that? I mean, one day he was bugging me and then — gone.

The worst were the "ifs." If only I'd been nicer to him. If only I'd paid more attention to him. If only I'd told him he was a good kid sometimes. If only I'd argued when Dad made Scotty — no, I wouldn't think about that . . . I couldn't.

There were times, lately, when I wanted to haul off and hit my father. He was like this big horsefly, jabbing and buzzing and making Mom pay bleary-eyed attention. And then, just when a spark of interest flickered in her eyes, he'd zoom off again. The ranch needed a ton of work, but even so, he seemed to be blind to everything else. He *knew* what Scotty's death had done to Mom. Why wasn't he doing more about it?

"You'll see, Jess," he said once when I'd tried to talk to him calmly and sensibly. "Fresh air, activity, the great outdoors, getting away from Winnipeg — these things will get Jeanie back to her old self. You'll see, Jess. Just you watch."

Well, I was watching. We'd been here four weeks. It was a good thing Winny was here. I didn't have a clue how to run a guest ranch and Mom would definitely look a little weird serving up dinner in an ancient housecoat and flannel PJs.

"Jess! Get out here!"

I didn't move. How long would it be before Wonder

Cowboy screwed up and fell flat on his face in the brown Alberta soil? Without Mom to watch over him, it was bound to happen.

❧ ❧ ❧

Willow Creek Ranch, Alberta, 1908, May 5
I, Ian Shaw, have decided to begin another account of the events in this house because I must somehow put away from me — with words — the anger that I feel. I am filled with it. I can feel it deep in my bones, blackening my heart. *She* has taken my other journal and destroyed it. It is gone — up through the chimney of our stone fireplace to float around the dark pine and rocky hills. Maybe it whispers into the ears of the birds and deer that live free in that bright air. Perhaps they look back at the little ranch house and know there is a prisoner within. Maybe they feel some sadness for me.

Everything on those lost pages is etched in my brain and will not be forgotten. *Or forgiven.*

I know that I am taking a chance beginning once more and I must always write quickly and furtively, for I mustn't be caught again. Fortunately, I have found a hiding place which not even *She* can find. Instead of doing my school work the other day, I stood with my forehead pressed against my window, dreaming out across the wood — riding my phantom steed up to the rocky foothills beyond. Somehow, the nib fell from the pen in my hand. For the life of me I could not find it. Only by chance did I glance down and see a space between the window sash and the wall. With my penknife, I worked away until I was able to create a long slot. By tying a string to the cover of my journal, I was able to lower the thin book down into the safe darkness between the inner and outer wall. Now, with careful manoeuvering, I can hide it quickly and easily, before pushing the flimsy board back into place. Only the tiny bit of string wound around a nail gives anything away. I have pushed my desk closer to the window, as well. The newly hired Indian woman, Madeline, cleans my room now and if she found it, I know she wouldn't tell. She's a game one and I quite like her. Her eyes smile.

It's hard to believe that last night at this very time I was anxiously waiting for Father to return from Calgary, where he was buying trail-hardened cattle driven all the way up from Montana. He arrived at the ranch just at twilight, dust churning under the bellies of the nervous beasts he was herding with the help of two of our neighbour's lads. One of the boys, Bill Parks, is only thirteen but he is almost as big as a man, while I, at fourteen, am as small as any sickly nine year old.

I almost fell out of my open window searching the milling riders and beasts for the glimpse of the gift Father had promised me. I must tell you that my heart soared—*soared!*—when I saw the small dapple-grey horse tied to the pommel of Father's saddle. It was frightened, its head rearing up, fighting the line of rope that held it captive. My heart went out to it. The sky was a pale yellow filtered through the rising dust, and in the middle of it all, the grey seemed to appear and disappear like an apparition. Was I dreaming? No. It was real. It *was* real! The little horse was there. My horse! I felt as if my chest would burst with a loud explosion of pure joy. It had happened. Father had done it! It had been a secret he and I had kept for weeks. Now, *She* would have to accept it.

I could hardly hold onto my canes, for my arms would not stop shaking. When I reached the stairs, I bumped slowly down each tread, trying hard to keep my walking sticks from thumping on the uncarpeted wood. I didn't want *Her* to know I was coming downstairs without her permission. I would surprise Father, who always comes through the front door to wait for dinner in the little parlour beside the kitchen.

As I made my way into the parlour, I could hear *Her* in the kitchen, scolding Madeline. If they happened to glance into the room, I would be hidden from view by the large winged sides of Father's chair. I waited for what seemed an eternity, feeling almost dizzy with the excitement of it all. What would she say? What would she do? I almost laughed out loud a few times and had to cover my mouth with both hands.

But the front door did not squeak open as it usually does. Instead, Father surprised me by appearing through the door that led from the kitchen.

He walked with the stiff-legged roll of a rider who has spent long days and nights in the saddle. He brought with him the wonderful odours of leather, horse and cattle. He had washed hastily, his neck still streaked with wet brown dust. He, too, looked surprised — to find me sitting hot-faced and grinning in the wide horsehair chair in front of the fire. Instead of striding forward and swinging me up into his arms as he often did, he stayed where he was, those arms hanging straight down at his sides. That's when I felt something drop inside of me with a sickening lurch. What was wrong? I knew *She* might arrive at any moment from the kitchen, where she and Madeline were preparing food for the tired riders, so I spoke quickly, pressing for news of the little grey horse.

Father hesitated, his eyes searching the room, as if for a way to escape. He opened his mouth to speak but, after saying my name, shut it again. Then *She* walked in. Father shook his head, gave me a beseeching look filled with pain, and strode from the room. A few seconds later, the front door slammed.

She stood in front of the fireplace, her back to the flames, cutting off most of the light and the warmth — her face a black mask of shadow, her tightly coiled hair and rigid stance outlined by the firelight.

"It simply won't do, Ian," she said. "It's just not on. I've told you this before. You're just not capable of handling a horse. Your father was very foolish to go against my wishes. He has sent the horse over to one of the neighbours' and from there it will be sold. I am doing this for your own good, Ian."

And then she added, "Off to bed you go. We have got a lot of new school work to cover in the morning."

I sat very still, staring at the toes of my woollen slippers, a great anger filling me up. I am very good at covering my feelings. *She* never allows emotions to be displayed and that is one thing I have learned from her. I gripped the arms of the chair until I thought the bones in my fingers would crack. Slowly, lifting my chin a little bit at a time, I forced myself to look at her. Did her hands tighten on each other as she looked back into my eyes? Had she read what was in them?

With my gaze still upon her, I felt for my walking sticks. When she reached forward to take my arm, I swung one of them up hard and fast. The swish of its movement through the air was as sure as a pistol-shot warning. The line of its blackness quivered in the dusky light between us. I wanted to strike her dead. For the first time ever, she stepped back from me.

Now, as I sit here scribbling, my hands shake and the pen slides in my slippery fingers. I must decide what to do. I must fight back, or this dreadful poison will surely do me in. Tonight when I lie in my bed I shall chart my course. I feel a new strength writing these words down. I can do it. For as Alan Breck says in *Kidnapped*, "Am I no' a bonny fighter?"

CHAPTER 2

MOM GOT UP FROM THE TABLE AND REACHED INTO a cupboard for a mug.

Pointing at the pile of foil-wrapped packages on a long side-table, she asked, "What are those?"

I sighed. "Winny and I were making them up yesterday when you came down for a drink of milk. Remember? It's bread and cakes for the overnight camp. Winny'll be here soon to wrap up the meat and stuff. That cleaning woman Dad hired should be here soon, too."

Mom thought a moment. "You mean the horrible little person with a name like a vegetable?"

I smiled. "Yeah, Lettice. She's going to help Winny and me get the stuff ready. Dad and Percy leave first thing tomorrow morning with the guests."

She frowned. "But aren't these — these guests arriving today?"

"Later this afternoon. But they don't go out until the morning. Dad's pretty hyper, bullying everyone, as usual."

"Hyper? He'll love every minute of it. I'm just glad... what's his name... Percy?... will be going along. I like the old fellow. And I'm glad your dad is having such a good time. He—Glen needs it."

I stared at her. "*He* needs it? Jeez, Mom, how come it's always you thinking about what *he* needs? Isn't it enough that he thinks about himself first? Did he ask us if we wanted to come here to live? No. Do you have to... jeez... I mean..."

But I'd already lost her. She reached for a piece of dry toast. "I'm going to lie down. I—I feel kind of light-headed."

She swung her empty cup vaguely in the air and looked around for the teapot.

"Look, Mom, I didn't mean to get mad at you, okay?" I said, pouring her a cup of strong tea. "It's just that—"

A distant shout cut me off. Why couldn't he leave me alone?

Mom looked down into her tea. "Yes. Well. There's your dad now. You'd better get outside. I'll just go back to bed for a little while. That's what I'll do. When Winny gets here, call me. I'll give you both a hand. We've got to clear out some of the stuff in the house, too—spring clean or something, don't we?" She looked around listlessly. "Are the guests' cabins ready?"

"Winny and Lettice and I did them," I said wearily. "Don't worry. I'll give Dad a hand for a while, but then I'll make sure I help Winny."

She smiled, a small flick of a thing, and turned away. "That's good, dear. Yes, that's good, but you call me when Winny comes anyway, okay?"

"Okay."

I watched her shuffle out in her big wool socks, the old pink housecoat trailing along the plank floor. There would be no point in calling her when Winny came. I knew she wouldn't come down. I wanted to holler at her to pull herself together, but instead I walked outside. The screen slapped shut. Sometimes I felt as tight as the coil spring on that door.

Hooves thudding the turfy ground echoed through the heavy air. The horses were after the oats Dad would have poured into the wooden troughs under the trees. I was glad there were rail fences and a wide dirt yard between me and those pounding creatures. Pulling in a deep breath, I sat down on the wooden steps and forced myself to relax.

The smell of the morning was damp and green, like newly mown grass. Sunlight struggled to pierce the dense tall pines surrounding the ranch. The fog, which was clearing in the open spaces, clung in thin white scarves around the skinny poplar trees in the corrals, but hung thick and still in the low areas.

I wanted Percy to get here. He seemed able to calm Dad down better than anyone. I listened for his and Winny's pick-up, but the gravel road was silent behind its pale skirt of swirling mist.

"Jess! Where the devil are you? Get over here and give me a hand, damn it!"

I started towards the corrals, scuffing the gravel under my boot heels. I generally worked with the horses when they were tethered, helping Percy groom them and nervously feeding them carrots and sugar lumps, but I hated when they became a milling, stomping, snorting crowd. Especially when my father got in amongst them, shouting and pushing. It put the horses — and me — on edge.

Dad had been a member of the R.C.M.P. Musical Ride a million years ago, and he rode his horse, Cocoa, like a madman. Percy, partly because of his age and arthritis, but mostly because he was Percy, rode the way he did everything—slow, easy and calm. He could settle down even the most skittery horse in two seconds.

The first week at the ranch, I'd ridden around a few times on a big brown and white patchwork of a horse called Slowbobs. He was an old guy, and we'd walked up and down the gravel road, having a good time. But Dad wanted me to help him with the pony trekking, so he'd found me a horse better suited to the Daughter of the Regiment. I should have known the big black monster was trouble when he tried to nip Dad while he was saddling him. The horse's name was Serenity.

The big brute had been fairly controllable as long as we were riding away from the ranch, but when he realized we were headed home, there was no holding him. I'd bounced around like a jelly baby until he'd swerved sharply at the open corral gate—without me. I'd landed on my back on the stony ground a hundred miles below, the air whooshed right out of my lungs. I was sure I was going to die.

Percy had run out of the stables and was bending over me, patting and clucking, when Dad came riding up, Serenity in tow.

"What in the hell did you think you was doin' puttin' the girl on that two-bit crazy?" he barked at Dad. "If I'da bin here, there's no way that little thing woulda been set up on that no-good excuse for a horse. I warned you about him, damn it!" Gently he helped me up. "You okay there, Jessica?"

I was gasping and choking but finally getting some air. Percy swore at Dad again. I was afraid Dad would fire him on the spot, but instead, he just sat back in his saddle and laughed.

"She's been paddling around in the shallows with that old crock, Slowbobs. In R.C.M.P. training camp, they taught us to swim by throwing us in the deep end. And they taught us to ride by putting us on the toughest horses. If I can do it, she can do it. She's always going on about girls being as good as boys. You don't learn to ride without a few falls." He swept one arm through the air. "We've all fallen. You just climb back up and get on with it. That Serenity is a good horse. I know as much about horseflesh as you do, Percy, my friend."

Percy looked up at him for a long time before spitting a brown stream of tobacco juice into the dust between Cocoa's feet. She danced a bit and Dad had to rein her in. Then Percy shifted the lump of tobacco to the other side of his mouth and wiped his yellowing moustache before taking me gently by the arm and leading me to the house. Winny spent the next hour applying icy poultices to my back and neck — and bad-mouthing Dad. The combination made me feel a whole lot better.

Even so, I could hardly move for a week. Doctor Ambrose told Dad I'd strained all the muscles in my back and chipped a bone in my left elbow. Then he gave Dad a lecture. It made me brave enough to announce that I wasn't going to ride again.

"I'll look after the horses in the corral and the sick ones in the barn, but no one is getting me back up on a horse."

Dad smiled knowingly and said, "This is just your way of getting even with me, isn't it? Come on. Admit it."

It was partly true, but I was also scared stiff at the thought of falling again. I answered him by walking away.

Nothing more was said until yesterday, during his coffee break. I was helping Winny peel potatoes.

"I realize now that you don't want to ride because you're afraid," he'd said, using his Patient Father voice. "But you can't run away from things just because you get hurt. You can't act like a wimpy girl now, can you, eh, love? You were so keen on riding. That's all you could talk about on the trip here."

A lie. We'd hardly talked at all across the prairies, but I had admitted — once — during the drive that the idea of riding a horse seemed okay.

I shrugged and scraped at a potato. "I don't care. You can't make me ride if I don't want to."

"You'll miss out on a lot of fun, kiddo," he coaxed. Then, reading the look on my face, his tone changed. "Don't think you'll win this one, young lady. I need you to help me run this place. And you'll do it on top of a horse, not as some beauty-parlour assistant to Percy. I can't afford to hire more people."

That made me see red. "Yeah. Right! You had a perfectly nice guy helping you and Percy. Remember Mr. Johnson? But you kept pushing him around — go here, go there, do this, do that, no please and no thank you — so he quit. He lasted two weeks. Well, I can't be pushed, see? Not like Mr. Johnson. And not like Scotty."

I felt my whole head buzz when I realized what I'd said. I'd promised myself I'd never bring it up. And I'd done it — letting Dad know what I thought of him pushing Scotty into that camping trip. There was a dark angry part, deep inside me, that wanted to hurt him for what he'd done to Scotty. And Mom. And me.

Dad's face tightened, the cheekbones standing out white and rigid under his tanned skin. Something in his eyes made me look away. I went back to my potato, scraping hard and quick. By the time I looked up again, he was gone. I just kept scraping until the potatoes were done and my injured elbow was burning with pain. Then I went to my room, turned my tape deck on full blast, and flung myself on the bed.

Now, in the mist, as I walked slowly towards the corrals, I told myself to climb over the fence and give him a hand, or he'd be impossible for the rest of the day. I had just reached the rails when two horses, tails high, manes flying, galloped along the far fence and swerved into the corral, followed closely by three others. Horses on the run look as if they'll pound right through you. I backed quickly off the log railing.

"Jess! Where the hell are you?" Dad yelled from behind one of the log outbuildings. He came into sight and swung his arm in the air. "Two of them are getting away again. For Pete's sake, get over here and shut the gate."

As I climbed the rail fence I spotted Dad's horse, Cocoa. She was limping. Most of the horses were contentedly snorting and munching, their noses deep in the troughs. I walked in a wide arc around them, grabbing Cocoa's halter as she hobbled by. An ugly flap of torn skin above a back hoof had turned into a gooey mass of blood, dirt and swarming flies.

"Damn it! Will you get over here, Jess!"

"Oh, hold onto your shirt!" I called back. "Cocoa's got a huge cut on one of her ankles. It looks pretty bad. Come 'ere."

"How many times do I have to tell you, it's fetlock. Fetlock! Not ankle. You sound like a bloody tin horn."

"Fetlock? Tin horn?" I muttered to Cocoa. "Jeez, soon I'll have to call him Pa." She looked over her shoulder at me and blew gently into my hair. I jumped, but laughed and patted her dusty flank. She was a pretty horse, with smooth brown hair and four white socks. Too bad she got stuck with Dad.

He appeared on the half-run, and we bent down to look

at her leg. He threw his hat on the ground and cursed loudly. I stepped back fast.

"Damn! What a mess! It would be the bloody lead horse. *My* horse! Cocoa, you idiot, what the devil have you done to yourself?" Dad scuffed the ground with his boots and swore again. "Where the devil is that Percy?" Then he turned on me, just as I knew he would. "What did you do? Drag her through the bloody gate?"

"She came in on her own, really slow, favouring that leg. Don't you look at *me* for someone to blame. You can see it's been this way for hours. I bet you went charging off the trail again last night. You sure took off from here in a cloud of dust. Showing us what a hot rider you are!"

There was a moment's hesitation before his face darkened. "Now *you look here*, Jess. I'm doing my best to start a business and you are *not* helping. Since we've arrived here, all you've done is fight me. This is a very important weekend and you are deliberately—"

I stopped listening. It was going to be the same old thing. Grow up. Take on responsibility. We're in this together. Your attitude is your big problem. On and on, forever and ever, amen. I'd promised myself that I would walk away from every fight and that's exactly what I did.

"Jess! Don't you take off now, young lady—whoa, Cocoa, it's okay girl, whoa there—Jess, you get back here, damn it!"

But I kept going.

"That's fine," he bellowed. "You're no good to me anyway. I'll take care of this myself."

I stepped behind the tack shed and leaned against the log wall. I didn't care what he thought. Nothing I ever did was right, but then, no one else did anything right by his standards, either. He'd been energetic and loud as far back as I could remember, but lately he was positively manic.

Where could I go? Into the kitchen—listening to the silence? If I went to my own room, I'd have to stare at an unmade bed and a stack of unpacked boxes filled with books, clothes and memories of home in Winnipeg. And of Scotty. What I needed right now was a good loud dose of Winny Eldridge.

Winny. I have to smile when I think about Winny. Did I mention she was bossy? We are talking here about the all-time superstar of bossy. She has grey hair that looks like the old joke about putting a bowl on your head and then hacking away. Her heavy face is as shiny smooth and red as a polished apple. She's taller than Dad and a lot heavier. She looks like she could take Percy and break him in two. She always wears slacks, a short-sleeved blouse that hangs over her hips, and white lace-up nurse's shoes with brightly coloured socks. I think she's the only person who scares Dad. He always wears a nervous grin around her. It gives me a kick.

She'd arrived that first day, taken one look at Mom, and told me—not *asked* me, *told* me—that it was up to her and me to get this place ready, and by heck we would. Then she'd leaned over and rested a huge square hand on Mom's shoulder.

"If that's all right with you, Missus," she'd said, her Foghorn Leghorn voice dropping to a soft roll.

The relief and gratitude on Mom's face had squeezed my heart.

After Mom had gone upstairs to lie down, Winny put her hands on her hips and nodded sadly. "We'll do it for her, eh? She looks done in." And that's exactly what we did. We did it for Mom.

Winny knew about Scotty but, after making her announcement, she didn't ask any questions. I liked that about Winny. And it made me even more certain that she was keeping a close watch over Mom. And me. For some reason, I knew Winny understood what I was going through, that she could see how lonely I was—how I felt that Mom and Dad had forgotten me—how everything made me feel sad and angry and desperate all mixed together.

I pushed myself off the wall and walked quietly away from the curses floating over from the corral. My boots led me down the grassy slope towards the gravel road.

The house was about eighty feet away, the open veranda angled towards the yard. I was about to skirt around the curve of the dirt drive when I got the tingly feeling I was being stared at. At the same time, it was as if a heavy cloud had suddenly passed across the early morning sun. My feet slowed down. I looked up towards Mom's window.

A slight figure stood at it, still and watchful.

Squinting my eyes to get a clearer view, I walked a little closer, then waved hesitantly. The small white face moved away from the window and the lace curtain dropped. I felt a cold chill wash over me. There were no curtains on Mom's windows; she had a plain blind. Where had those lace curtains come from?

A loud voice carried over from the corral. "Not *another* messed-up horse! That's *all* I need! Jess! Go call Percy and tell him to get a move on. Jess? Where is that damn Percy!"

Dad's shouting brought me back to earth. The shadow lifted. There, just as always, was the strip of Mom's pull-down blind with its long tassel. It must have been a trick of the light that created the lace curtains—that made Mom look so much like a little kid. Yes, I was sure of it now.

Even so, I walked away without looking back — just in case that hovering white face at the window had returned.

❦ ❦ ❦

Willow Creek Ranch, Alberta, 1908, May 9
This morning it was quite cold and I sat alone at my bedroom window watching Father and the hired men working below. Fog misted the land. The cattle that had been crowded into the corrals bawled and steamed, their sides and massive shoulders pushing against the rail fences. Branding day at last. I could see Father amongst the other men, flushed with pride. It has taken a long time, but Father's patient wait has ended. He lost most of our stock last winter but now he can begin anew.

"This has been one of the worst and longest snowstorms John Parks has seen since he's been ranching," Father had said to *Her* that cold March morning after so many dead cows had been discovered. "I'll have to wire Father for more money. I'll need another fifty head of cattle at least, if I am to begin another breeding stock. My only consolation, and it is a grim one, is that everyone has had quite bad losses, Augusta."

She put down her teacup slowly. It clicked on the saucer. In an even tone, she said, "You lost your cattle, Nigel, because you aren't a rancher and you never will be. Why can't you simply face that very obvious fact?"

"I can learn to be a good rancher," Father said stiffly. "It's what I want to do."

"What you *want* to do and what you are *capable* of doing are two different things," she snorted. "You are the son of an Anglican bishop, with an education in classics, *not* cattle."

"It doesn't matter," he said, his voice bitter. "I watched my father do what he was capable of, as you put it, and he has been unhappy every day of his life. He wants me to be happy."

"And are you happy, Nigel? *I'm* not happy. *I'm* not at all happy."

Father sighed. "We planned for this together. It takes time to build a life out here. It could be a good life. You agreed, Augusta."

"Because I thought you'd soon weary of it. It doesn't matter. It will soon be over and we can go home. I keep your father up to date with our miserable life here in this wretched wilderness. I have told him everything about these five long years, Nigel. I don't think you'll get any more money out of him."

Father stood up, his face ashen. "You will never understand my father or me." And with that, he left the room.

After Grandfather sent the money all the way from Edinburgh, *She* wouldn't talk to either of us for days, except to make me work harder at my school work and to lecture me on the need for a sound, practical education.

This morning, as I watched Father working below, I wondered about Father and *Her*. He may have his cattle, but she has the greater will. Hadn't I been reminded of that once again when my grey horse was taken away — without a word from Father on my behalf?

I spend a lot of time staring out of my window, watching the dark hills that ring the lower pasture. I love this view. But today the sight of it hurts me. I will never ride through those shadowy trees which are now enticingly striped with warming yellow sunlight. My heart aches, for today I am not sitting on my beautiful grey watching the branding, as Father had promised.

In the days after the grey was sold, I was filled with feelings I couldn't control. At times, it was as if I was slipping deeper and deeper into thick black mud.

Today, as I watched the bustle below, something swelled inside my chest, something I didn't want to examine too closely, in case, by touching it, I caused it to explode through my skin. I had the certain feeling that if that happened, I'd collapse, like a pillow emptied of sharp black feathers. The few tears that squeezed out of my eyes hurt, as if being branded on my face. I wiped them away quickly. I would never allow *Her* to know that I had weakened.

Before she demanded the sale of my horse, I'd always obeyed her, working at this small wooden desk, knowing that as long as I worked hard, the truce would continue. But today, as I turned away from the brightness of the early morning outside to the brown dullness of my room and the smell of ink and paper, my soul sickened. I looked at the neat pages of algebra equations that I had copied earlier in the week. Today, I was to complete three pages of them by our midday meal. I dipped my pen into the ink. Holding it over the page, I watched a dark shiny ball of thick liquid tremble on the tip of the nib. I remembered her words: "It simply won't do, Ian. It's just not on. You're just not capable of handling a horse." The ink landed like a black sunburst on the paper.

It was easy after that. I made sure that each answer was exactly one number out. I scraped and smeared the pages, drawing some figures large and others so tiny I could hardly form their shapes. I broke three nibs. I must confess I felt a clutch of fear when I realized what I was doing. At the same time, an exhilaration at my boldness overwhelmed that fear. Now, the awful tiredness I have felt for so much of each day is gone.

I know that she will soon come and take away my day's work to examine at her leisure. I must put this journal away. She mustn't find it. I will take out the harmonica Father bought in Calgary to replace the one *She* threw away to discipline me. I will play the one song she insists I not play, for she says it is too common. And that, of course, is why I shall play it!

CHAPTER 3

THE HAZE ALONG THE ROAD WAS CLEARING BUT THE deep ditches on either side, thick with tall grasses and humped willow bushes, were still heavy with mist. My boots crunched over the gravel. Winny and Percy would be along any minute, Winny driving hell for leather, Percy sitting beside her, chewing tobacco bulging his thin cheek. If they saw me, I'd catch a lift back.

About a quarter of a mile along, I stopped. Music? At first it was a tinny sound, like a distant whistle. But as I listened, it grew in tone and clarity. Yes... a harmonica. The sad little tune drifted through the heavy air. A shiver ran across my shoulders like a daddy longlegs.

I was sure I saw something moving just ahead of me, behind a swirling wall of fog—a grey or white horse? Had one of ours escaped? I was positive I could hear soft whinnying sounds under the melody of the harmonica.

"Hello?" I called out, my voice tremulous.

Abruptly, the music stopped and the fog vanished, as if wiped away by a huge hand. I let out a strangled giggle when I saw the silvery trunk of a poplar close to the road.

Some horse! Even so, I couldn't shake the goose-bumping uneasiness that had gripped me.

A few seconds later, I heard a different sound. A swish-swash mixed with a regular wet plop, plop, plop—coming along the ditch. Suddenly, something appeared out of the mist to my left. A pointed nose and two shiny eyes were followed by a small black and white body. When I laughed out loud, the border collie stared at me, its ears shifting, as if trying to decide whether to bark an alarm. Right behind the dog appeared a big brown bobbing head, then a broad tawny chest, brown leather gloves, a quilted plaid shirt and a black Stetson. When it all came together into a horse and rider, they too stopped to stare.

The rider was about seventeen or eighteen. His face was angular and dark-skinned with a thin mouth and short nose. In the shadow of the hat's brim, his eyes narrowed into slits. Long legs wore jeans and dirty, well-worn leather chaps.

I patted the dog, who moved its bony head under my hand, eyes half shut with pleasure. The rider clicked his tongue and the big brown horse stepped forward, one eye rolling sideways to keep me in its field of vision.

I looked up at the boy. "Hi," I said.

He nodded, then turned his attention to the dog. "Get goin' there, Prue. Don't hang about." The dog looked back, her eyes soft and pleading. "You heard me. Get."

I lowered my hand and touched her nose. She gave me an apologetic lick before bounding up to the boy and horse. All of them moved away together. I turned and watched them until the mist closed around the horse's swaying backside and flicking tail.

"Nice to meet you, too," I called out sarcastically.

Who the heck was that, I wondered? Stuck-up snob. And what was he doing on our property?

The answer came a few minutes later when Winny braked beside me in a cloud of dust.

"Hey there, Jess. Almost ran you down. What are you doing way out here, for Pete's sake?" she said, leaning out the pick-up window.

"Dad's on the rampage. I had to get away before I knocked him out with the manure shovel."

"Had an idea he'd be full of vinegar and heartburn this morning," muttered Winny. "Percy'll settle him."

Percy was in shadow, but I could see from the stiff way he sat that his arthritis was acting up.

"Hi, Percy. Bad today, huh?"

"Yeah," he said slowly, raising one twisted hand, "it's botherin' me some with this cold damp. I'll loosen up as the day goes on. I think Winny's bein' too hopeful about your dad. He's goin' to be pretty put out with me. Won't be able to go along tomorrow like I promised."

Winny's voice boomed around the inside of the cab. "Who cares? You can't work and that's that. For cripe's sake!" She turned to me and boomed out the window. "We told your dad we'd look for another hand when things got busy. Now's as good a time as any. Got Ben Hodge to try out. Next to Percy, he's the best in the county and knows these hills like the back of his hand. He and Percy have spent many a day up in those mountains together."

She leaned further out of the window and looked behind her. "Lettice'll be along soon. We passed the great cyclist a while back. Asked if she wanted a lift, but she views the five miles from that cabin of hers as some great challenge. Bright as a penny. Told us it would probably rain before the day was out. Always cheeriest when she's got bad news."

I laughed. "Yesterday she told me she was always falling off that bike now, but that was only because her son had

32

ridden it down the creek bed and skewed the front wheel. Said he'd made a mile and a half before falling off and breaking his arm."

"Idiot," Winny snorted. "Did you see Ben by any chance, Jess? He'd be riding his own horse, a dark bay called Bower."

I nodded. "He passed me a second ago. With a little dog. Just stopped, stared and went on by. Didn't even say hi."

"That's our boy," she said, grinning. "Don't expect small talk from Ben. It just isn't in him. But he's a good kid. We'd better catch up so his lordship — I mean, your dad — doesn't run the kid off his property. Ben'll take Percy's pay for the trip. Then after your dad sees how good he is, we'll talk about him filling in for Percy on all the big rides. Of course, your dad'll think it's his own idea." She winked and rumpled my hair. Good thing I wear it real short — she does that all the time.

"Hop in the back, there, Jessica," said Percy.

I lowered the tailgate, jumped in and hung on tight. Winny took off like a stock-car racer and we arrived just as Ben Hodge was tying his horse to a post in the middle of the yard. Winny helped Percy out of the truck, but when his feet hit the dirt he gently pushed her aside, hitched up his jeans, and hobbled over to Ben. Together they walked slowly past the tack house towards the corrals full of fly-bothered animals and a crazy man waiting to give someone — anyone — a good tongue-lashing.

"Percy looks like he can hardly move," I said worriedly. "Will he be okay?"

Winny humphed and shook her head. "Nothing'll stop that man until he's dead and buried. But," she added with a sigh, "as long as he's busy, he's happy, pain or no pain. Come on. I'll make your mom a nice cup of tea before Miss

Loony Lettice arrives. I could use one myself." She peered at me from under grey, bristling brows. "Your dad does know that you're working with me during this weekend stint, right?"

"I've told him at least ten times, but... " I shrugged.

"Well, never mind, I'll make it clear if he gives us any hassle. You do *not* want to ride. Am I right?"

I nodded firmly. "Right."

We were sitting on the back stairs eating sticky ginger-bread and swilling tea when Lettice wobbled into the yard on her rusty bike, the front tire flopping with each turn.

Lettice is this chronically cheerful, disorganized, tatty bag of bones who lives in a log cabin that once belonged to her grandmother. She has four kids, between seven and twelve years old, all of them crammed in that tiny shack. Winny, who used to be a schoolteacher, once referred to Lettice's kids as "babies of murky origin." I think she meant Lettice didn't have any idea who the fathers were.

Today Lettice wore a washed-out blue sundress and a pair of oversized sandals. Her toes, slathered in bright orange nail polish, stuck out of the dusty ends. With her scrawny arms and flat chest and all those freckles, she looked like a starving kid. Only when you saw the criss-crossed lines in her pixy face did you realize that she was middle-aged.

"Whewee!" she said, leaning her bike against the side of the house and wiping her forehead with an exaggerated flourish. "I thought I wasn't going to make it. Some guy just about clipped me with his Jeep. People get hit by cars all the time riding bikes, did you know that?" She grinned cheerfully, showing nicotine-stained teeth. "If it was a hit-and-run, I coulda been lying on that dirt road for hours until someone come along. And a'course they mighta driven right over me." She contemplated a moment, then said, "But I'da been dead, so I wouldn'ta felt it, would I? Which is probably just as well. I'd like a nice funeral with lots of wild roses coverin' my coffin. 'Course I'd have to die when the roses are out — but I'd like that okay."

"We'll make sure we bump you off next summer, Lettice," said Winny, elbowing me in the ribs. "Meanwhile, as long as you're still breathing, how about a nice chunk of gingerbread cake?"

Lettice pointed at the piece in my hand. "Not as big as that. Them spices and all that sugar can bung you up pretty good, but a cup of tea will help, no doubt."

Help what? I had no idea. She plunked herself down on the bottom step, stretching out her skinny legs. Then she lit a cigarette from a flattened package she dug out of her sundress pocket.

Winny handed her a mug of tea and a small piece of gingerbread, which Lettice eyed suspiciously before shoving the whole thing into her mouth. She looked up at us as if she was going to say something really important just as soon as she'd got all of it down her scrawny gullet.

But Winny didn't give her the chance. "Well, ladies, let's get to work," she said. "Lettice, no smoking in the house."

Lettice nodded happily. She took a final drag before putting the tip of her cigarette out in the dirt and carefully storing the butt in the compressed package. As I reached inside the door and grabbed the master key-ring for the cabins, I glanced back at the corrals. Ben Hodge was moving confidently amongst the horses, laying a gloved hand on each neck as he passed by. I wasn't sure I'd ever talk to *that* particular person again, considering his rudeness. But if he got the job, Dad might just possibly stay off my back.

I sighed happily. With Winny's booming orders and Lettice's crazy ramblings and all the hard work to do, I would get through this day just fine — I wouldn't even have much time to think about my mother lying upstairs staring at the ceiling. And I would also forget the face at the window and the strange music on the road.

Suddenly, from nowhere, a cold chill wrapped around me, cutting through the rising heat of the morning. A small sigh, faint but penetrating, breathed in my ear. I scrambled through the door, banging it shut behind me.

❦ ❦ ❦

Willow Creek Ranch, Alberta, 1908, May 9
I am writing this by candlelight. Earlier this evening, I lay in bed, pretending to read by the lowering sun that cast its yellow glow over my pages. In fact, I was waiting. For *Her*. What would she say about the ink-splattered pages?

She is a cool one, no mistake. She walked straight into the room and threw my work in the wastebasket beside my desk.

"I cannot understand why you felt compelled to do something as silly as this," she said, her voice brittle. "You show a childishness that doesn't suit a boy of your intelligence or age. I am more embarrassed for you than angry. Now that you have this tantrum out of your system, I expect to see the very same work done properly. By tomorrow evening at the latest."

With that, she walked out of the room, her heels tapping briskly down the hall. I crept out of bed and gently closed my door. Under the covers again, I lay shivering. Would I be brave enough to have another "tantrum" tomorrow and the day after and the day after that?

Perhaps I should stop, I told myself. After all, I'd made my point, hadn't I? I shook my head in anger. How could I think like that? If I admitted defeat, *She* would be the winner.

Night dropped suddenly over our valley. Usually, the time between crawling into bed and falling asleep is the best part of the day. It is the only time that is truly mine. I closed my eyes, trying to conjure up my other world.

She can't see inside my brain, I reminded myself. She can't control my thoughts. I am still Ian Alexander Shaw. And my thoughts are my own, and no one can intrude.

I knew I was fooling myself.

In that other world — that wonderful place — I could ride across long golden fields, up shadowed hills, and across brightly splashing streams. Sometimes, I would be alone with my horse, and sometimes, I had my friend with me. He didn't have a horse. I had decided his parents wouldn't allow him one. So I would proudly ride up to the meadow behind his farm and whistle. He was always waiting for me — running out of the shadows of the silvery trees like a spirit ghost. I would reach down and take his hand and pull him onto the back of my powerful horse. Locked together, we would ride away. I hadn't given the boy a name. Maybe it is just as well. When you name someone, you miss them even more when they are gone. And surely he has gone now, the boy with the thin eager face.

I concentrated hard. Maybe it's not too late, I told myself, fighting down the fluttery panic in my chest. I concentrated hard. Maybe the boy and the horse are still there. If so, where shall we go tonight? To rescue a family in a burning house? To hunt with the Sarcee Indians that sometimes visit the ranch to barter? I managed to bring the phantom horse to dim life at the edge of my mind, but just as he began to form, he faded. Again and again I tried. Why, why couldn't I make him stay?

I know why. *She* has been able to push her way into my secret world. By selling my beautiful grey horse, she has destroyed it. How can one dream about something that has no possibility of coming true?

It is as if I am standing on a tiny island so flimsy that, at any moment, it might dissolve. The surrounding blackness tosses chill waves of despair over me. When this little island gives way, will the terrible darkness suck me up completely?

CHAPTER 4

W E STOPPED FOR LUNCH AROUND TWELVE-THIRTY.
The guests would be drifting in, Percy said, any
time between three o'clock and dinner.

"Most of them don't like to pass up Winny's cookin'. And
they know dinner is at six-thirty sharp."

Dad reached over and grabbed one of the sliced chicken
sandwiches we'd made. "I'll take a shower and change, just
in case some of them get here soon. Where's that kid Ben?
Isn't he having lunch? I didn't scare him off already, did I?"
He grinned.

Percy loaded two tin plates with sandwiches. "Ben don't
scare easy, Glen. I'll go eat with him. He's cleaning Cocoa's
leg."

Dad got the message. Quickly, he said, "I wasn't ignoring
it. I didn't want to touch it until the vet came. Speaking of
which, did you call him, Winny?"

Winny poured coffee into a couple of tin mugs. When
Percy was gone, she answered, "I called him all right. He'll
be here after lunch."

"Good. It's important that we . . . " His words trailed off.

I stopped cutting gingerbread and looked over my shoulder. Mom was standing in the doorway, blinking as if someone had turned on the lights while she was sleeping.

"Jeanie," Dad said, "come and have some lunch."

"What time is it?" Mom said softly. "Is it lunch already?"

I glanced at Dad. For the first time in weeks, we might be on the same wavelength. Surely he could see how out-of-it she was. But no, he pasted that stupid grin on his face—his let's-be-cheerful-for-Jeanie face. It usually came with a loud hearty voice.

"I'm not very hungry," Mom said. "I've been reading. The time just flew by." She looked at me. "Jess, you told me you'd call me when Winny arrived, but you didn't."

"I brought you a cup of tea, Missy, remember?" Winny said. "With gingerbread. Just as soon as I arrived."

Mom's hand flew up to her mouth. "Oh! That's right!" she said, and then she laughed, a tittery, brittle sound. "I must have been deep in my book. How silly."

Dad beamed at Mom. "Listen, love, how about coming down to greet the guests later? They'd like to meet you, I'm sure. Eh, love?"

Her eyes widened. "Oh, uh, no... I don't think so, Glen. Not this time. I—well—you know I hate meeting new people all in a bunch like that."

"I would *like* to think that you will take an interest in this enterprise of ours, Jeanie," he said slowly, looking down at his plate, the smarmy smile sliding off his face.

"Do you want some gingerbread, Mom?" I asked, realizing I was using the same hearty tone as Dad.

She was staring at him, her face white and frightened. "What? No... no thanks, Jess. I—uh— I'm going upstairs. Maybe Winny can bring me something in a bit."

"Of course," said Winny, glaring at Dad.

He ran a hand over his hair and grasped his neck, kneading it a couple of times. "Yeah, well, you do what you want, Jeanie." All pretence at cheerfulness was gone.

Mom's voice came out high and thin. "I can't do what I want, Glen. That's the problem. I can't *do* anything. I can't *do* what you want because ... because ... " She walked back through the doorway, muttering, "It doesn't matter. It just doesn't matter."

I bit my lip, waiting for Dad to call out to her, to go after her.

Instead, he slammed his palm on the table. "Well, I have things to do. I've got fifteen people coming for the weekend and I've got to see that it goes just right, don't I? Yes, sirree! I've got things to do. Who'll pay the bills, eh? Who — "

"I imagine *you* will, if we're lucky," Winny interrupted. "Here's the vet," she added. "He's just parked over by the barn. That'll give you something else to do."

Dad scowled, but she stuck her chin out and faced him down. In two strides he was out the door. I sank into a chair, my insides quivering.

Winny rested one hand on my shoulder for just a second. "Come on, kiddo. Help me get this garlic bread wrapped."

I nodded. We all had something to do. Except Mom. I got to work, but I felt in my gut that something pretty important had just happened. For the *first* time, Dad had shown impatience with Mom locking herself away. Would he start nagging at her? And for the first time, Mom had spoken out loud about how she was feeling. She hadn't said much, but whatever was going on behind those troubled eyes wasn't good. I was afraid for her.

The guests arrived in the afternoon. Winny and I had struck a bargain. I'd work hard behind the scenes and she would deal with the guests. The small log cabins, rough and simple though they were, had been scrubbed and polished. That morning we'd given the miniature bathrooms an extra lick with Spic and Span and put fresh towels on the racks. Even so, now and again, guests would saunter into the kitchen as if they owned it, looking for things like safety pins or film for their cameras. We had a small supply of stuff like that, and Winny and I were able to get rid of each snooper pretty quickly.

Lettice was only too happy to tell them how it would probably rain all weekend and how horseback riding was bad for the kidneys, that a bike was much safer — unless you drove down the middle of the road, and even then it was still safer than a horse. Why, just look at her cousin Ralphy, she told one stunned woman, he was never the same after that horse kicked him in the head when he was trying to take a stone out of its shoe. Why, he'd taken to wearing no clothes. Stark naked, he'd go. Ralphy, that is, not the horse. And, she added gravely, Ralphy was weird only on Sundays, which was the strangest thing because he'd never gone to church before the accident.

I had to run into the storage cupboard to howl quietly until my sides ached. When I managed to control things down to a few hiccupping giggles, I came out of the cupboard, but Winny shot me a look that sent me right back inside again.

I felt a lot better afterwards. Things started looking brighter. Maybe all Mom needed was a little more time. Sure, that had to be it. I was taking it all too seriously. Just a bit more time.

The dining room of the old house and the big parlour in the newer part had been set aside for the guests, and that's where Dad could be found all afternoon, telling funny stories, mixing drinks, and explaining the route that the group would take for the two days and one night they'd be out.

Lettice went home to her piles of animals and kids just before dinner. Winny and I worked like mad in the kitchen, dishing up soup and salad, baked beans with pineapple, pan-roasted potatoes and the apple pies Winny had baked the day before. They'd been prepared in the biggest pie tins I'd ever seen and we cut them into Paul Bunyan-sized slices and added chunks of old cheddar. Dad was responsible for the steaks on the barbecue pit. Later, while the guests drank coffee and filled the parlour and veranda with cigarette smoke and laughter, Winny and I slumped in the kitchen, legs splayed, hair damp, staring morosely at the piles of dirty plates.

"We'll do this lot and then we'll eat," said Winny, fanning herself with a crumpled piece of tin foil. "I, for one, will have to swallow one of those steaks whole. I'm too darn tired to chew."

"We'd like something to eat, too," said a crusty voice from the back door. "Before we drop from hunger."

"Didn't you eat at the buffet out there?" Winny demanded. "You always eat with the folks."

Percy walked into the room. Behind him, in the shadows, stood Ben Hodge. He nodded in my direction. Nice of him. But the smile he gave Winny made me straighten up in my seat.

"Mr. Locke said we should finish organizing the gear and then come in the back way to eat. So here we are." His voice was deep and rusty-sounding, as if he didn't use it much.

"Well, of all the — why, Percy, you've been eating in that dining room since 1960," said Winny. "Aren't you good enough to eat with His Highness?"

Percy must have seen my worried frown because he said, "Now, don't you give it a thought, Jessica. And Winny, don't you go gettin' on your high horse, neither. The man's runnin' his business the way he sees fit. I never did like mixing with those city types. They don't know the cost of hay and don't particularly care to. All they ever talk about are things with initials—CDs and BMWs and VCRs and the like. I'm happier sortin' gear than sitting in there with them. Let Glen Locke figure things out on his own." He threw his hat over on the counter and said, "Enough of this yakking. I need sustenance, woman!"

Winny heaved herself to her feet. "There's a few steaks left over. Jess, you stick 'em in a frying pan to reheat and I'll sort out the rest of the scraps the lords and ladies have left us. You move those dishes over there, Ben."

Ben stacked dirty dishes while I reheated the steaks. I watched him out of the corner of my eye. He kept his hat on until Winny reached over and flicked it from the back, tipping the brim over his eyes. He coloured a little and tossed it onto the counter beside Percy's. I think he muttered, "Sorry, Winny."

Winny handed him a full plate. He sat down and didn't say a word except, "Thanks." The plate she put in front of me was loaded with food. If this was scraps, it was okay by me. I dug in.

When Winny put Ben's second helping in front of him, something caught her attention. She wrapped her stubby fingers around his chin and turned his head towards her. There was an ugly red swelling on his forehead near the temple. Percy's hand tightened on his fork, turning the knobbly knuckles white. Ben just kept his eyes on his plate.

"When?" was all Winny asked.

Ben's voice was almost a mutter. "Just before I left this

44

mornin'. It's okay. It's nothin'.'"

What was going on here? Had Ben been in some sort of fight? Winny's face was as hard and tight as a drum. Before walking back to the stove, she ran her hand down the back of his head. She was mad at someone, but it obviously wasn't Ben. She muttered to herself while flipping steaks, the spatula trembling in her hands.

Finally, she sighed and in a brighter tone, said, "Well, except for my own plate, you two have practically cleaned out Mother Hubbard's cupboard. You may as well polish off these last two steaks."

Percy, in a gruffer voice than his usual one, said, "Plunk that meat right down with more of them beans, eh, Ben?"

Ben looked up and a slow smile stretched his narrow lips. "I could eat a bit more."

After that, we ate in a silence that seemed to hang like smoke. Just when it was getting painful, Winny dished up the pie and asked Percy about the outside preparations for the trail ride. According to him, everything was perking along just fine.

He slurped his coffee and looked at me from under wiry eyebrows. I always avoided looking at Percy's head when he had his hat off. That's because he wears a thick, black, glossy hairpiece square in the middle of his head. His own hair, curling around his neck and ears, is silvery grey. For the first week or so, I just couldn't look without feeling horror and pity. I soon learned there was nothing to pity about Percy. He wears the thing with such dignity. Even so, it looked to me as if some strange sleek animal had settled down on top of his head for a nap. I found it better to carefully avoid looking in case it got up and walked away.

"I guess your dad's told you what your job is tomorrow, eh, Jessica?" he asked.

45

I nodded. "You'll load the truck with those big metal pack boxes tonight and I'm to drive them to Webster's Corner at eleven tomorrow. Dad and ... er ... Ben will bring the pack horses and pick them up. Right?"

Percy smiled. "Right. They'll take the bedding and the first meal with them. One of those supply boxes has the camp stove and griddle, Ben, so you'll need two pack horses. Okay?"

Ben nodded. "Who's doin' the cooking tomorrow? You usually do it."

Winny spoke up. "Percy, you can get that look off your face. You are *not* going, and that's that. It'll be you or the boss, Ben. I've cooked most of it anyways. And the pancake batter — well, you've made that before. Directions are on the side of the packages. You'll manage."

"*You* work with the horses," Ben said to me. "Can't you ride?"

I shook my head and crumbled a bit of pie crust with my fork.

"When has she had time to learn?" said Winny. "If she isn't scrubbing her fingers to the bone getting the cabins shipshape, she's shovelling manure and polishing leather." When I looked up, she was glaring at me. "When I first met Percy I didn't know one end of a horse from the other. Scared to death of them, wasn't I, Perce?"

He opened his mouth to say something, but she went right on.

"That's what I was — scared to death. So don't let anyone bully you into getting back up on a horse until you're good and ready."

Percy looked at Winny and then at me. I knew she was lying to make me feel better. Winny scared of a mere horse? Never.

Percy nodded and finished off his coffee. "Well, Ben, Winny and I'll bed down over in Cabin Three like we always do when guests are here. You can stretch out in your sleeping bag on our floor."

Winny spoke up. "No need, Ben. Mr. Locke says you can bunk in one of the spare rooms in the new wing. That way you won't disturb the Missus. If you stay on, we'll sort out something else depending on what His Lordship wants. Maybe we can talk your mom into moving back near you, Jess, and Ben can take that poky little room of hers." She frowned at Percy. "As for you, you'll finally get to do the job of two men, instead of four. Ben'll be the other two."

Percy said, "If all goes well, there'll still be bigger groups comin' up. Locke'll need more than Ben and himself on those trails. I may still have to go along later on."

"We'll have to see, won't we?" she boomed. "He might be able to get a kid or two part-time. Maybe you can go along now and again. *Maybe*. But... now... well, I'm awfully glad that Ben will be around this weekend. You stay put, Percy. Let the boy show Mr. Locke what he's made of."

Percy knew when he was beaten. "Never marry a schoolteacher, Ben. They're too used to being the boss. Let's get these dishes out of the way. If we all work together, me and my sweetie can take a nice walk along the creek before we turn in."

Winny flushed right up to her straight grey bangs and pushed him gently with a big hand, but she didn't argue. We all worked—Winny washing, Percy sitting on a chair drying slowly and carefully, Ben scraping the dirty dishes, and I putting the clean ones away. While we clattered around, we heard the guests calling good night to one

47

another. Soon the big house was quiet.

"We need one of those industrial-sized dishwashers," said Winny, wiping damp hair off her forehead. "I'll bring it up with you-know-who when the time seems right. I'm getting too old for this. Jess, leave that. Go in the parlour and gather up the ashtrays and dirty glasses."

I grabbed a tray and dragged myself into the stuffy parlour. Dad was sitting hunched forward in one of the weird chairs we'd inherited with the place — made out of moose antlers and leather. His face, in the dying firelight, looked droopy and sad. But when I clinked the ashtrays, he sat up with a jerk.

"Well, Jess, we're off to a great start, eh?" he said loudly. "Tomorrow... adventure! You get busy and learn to ride and we'll make a great team. Then we can run this place the way it should be run. We'll have it paid off in no time."

What made me think he was sad? His eyes were crackling with his own brand of electric energy. With a sketch of a wave, he rushed off talking about a good night's sleep. As usual, he saw no point in asking me what I thought of his plans. What else was new? I slammed four overflowing ashtrays and three sticky glasses onto my tray and stomped back to the kitchen.

❧ ❧ ❧

Willow Creek Ranch, Alberta, 1908, May 12
At dinner tonight, Madeline brought in the serving dishes one by one and placed them on the snowy tablecloth. Silver gleamed and crystal sparkled in the lamplight.

When Madeline left the room, *She* sniffed and placed her napkin carefully on her lap. "I've tried and tried to make that woman understand that she must bring the dishes to the sideboard and serve each dish one by one. It's quite hopeless. She may have worked for those Gallaghers for a few years, but she learned absolutely nothing. No one in this wilderness knows how to lay a table or serve a decent meal. When I stayed with the Gallaghers last year, they ate no better than hogs at a trough."

On one of my rare outings this spring, I had been allowed to go to the Gallaghers' homestead with Father. We'd been invited for dinner, which was all light-hearted laughter and pots of Irish stew. They didn't mention my crippled leg and treated me in the same casual manner they treated their own small, yellow-haired boys.

Before moving to Canada, *She* had travelled with her doctor on his home visits around the English countryside, helping with birthings. The upper class had certain duties, she'd informed me, telling me how her own mother nursed the sick on their huge estate in Sussex.

"I knew if your father was going to become someone here in Canada, I'd have to take on these duties," she'd told me one day, when I'd asked her where she went for weeks at a time. "I assumed there would be many ladies like myself ... " here she'd paused, " ... gentlewomen, who would need proper care." Her face hardened. "The wealthy, it seems, go to a nursing home in Calgary well before their confinement. I am called upon to help lazy, slovenly girls give birth to puny little brats, one after another." She sniffed disdainfully. "That Mrs. Gallagher has been with child seven times and she's not twenty-five years old. Only the two boys lived. It's a disgrace."

I imagined five skinny little babies in tiny little coffins. Poor Mrs. Gallagher. Yet, despite these hardships, she is a jolly, freckle-faced woman with crackling red hair. I like her.

I don't imagine I'll see the Gallaghers again, because on my return home, I'd told *Her* what a good time I'd had with them. I haven't been allowed to visit since.

When Madeline placed the last dish, piled high with boiled potatoes, on the table, she looked shyly at Father.

"What a good-looking meal, Madeline," he said. "Thank you."

"Please, Nigel, don't talk to the servant as if she's one of *us*," *She* said, when Madeline had returned to the kitchen. "She won't answer, in any case. She barely says a word to me. A simpleton. When Ian gets back to England, he'll have to be taught all over again his position in life if you don't set a better example." She spoke in a crisp sharp voice.

I tried to eat but all I could think about were her words, "When Ian gets back to England." Why did she keep saying that? I didn't want to leave Alberta or the foothills. I couldn't leave Father. She was using the threat as another punishment for my defying her over the past three days. I stared at the gravy congealing on my dinner.

Slowly, I mashed the dark liquid into the potatoes with my fork. That was when she began another lesson on table etiquette. And as always, it was Father who was setting a bad example. I watched the thin lips talking, talking, talking — a stream of cutting snipes and insults. I kept my eyes on her all the time, making sure that she saw how I deliberately held my fork wrong, scraped my plate, chewed with my mouth open. When Madeline came in with our sweet, I loudly praised the apple pie. *Her* mouth grew tighter and tighter. When the meal was finally over, I asked Father to be excused and was surprised by something in his eyes — was he smiling?

"I'll be up to read to you soon, old chap," he said. "Just as soon as I've finished up in the barn. You get that book out and find our place. All right?"

I nodded, my eyes on *Her*. She was looking from one of us to the other, her slender neck seeming to stretch even longer, her chin in the air, her hooded eyes suspicious. I knew she had seen the wink he gave me. Now I have only to wait to see how she will show her displeasure. No doubt it won't take long.

CHAPTER 5

I STOOD UNDER THE HOT SHOWER, LETTING THE HEAVY beat of water pummel the tight muscles in my back. Winny had told Ben to use the bathroom at Dad's end of the long hallway, so I didn't need to hurry. Mom and I shared this one, just inside the newer part of the house, a few steps from the hall that led to the old wing, where she had chosen to sleep alone. Away from Dad. And me.

Suddenly, my throat hurt, the way it does when you fight tears. For sixteen years, she had come to my room and kissed me good night. When I was drowsy, she would gently remove the book from my hand and kiss my forehead, but if I was wide awake, we'd talk quietly together for a while. Since Scotty had died, she hadn't come into my room once. Sometimes I was sure she was mad at me for still being around, when he was gone forever. Grief paralyzed me, until the pounding water turned cold.

Towelling dry, I yanked on my pyjamas and ran down the hall to my room. I crawled under the covers and stared through the far window at the darkening sky, forcing myself to think of practical things, blinking back the tears waiting just behind my eyelids. The smell of rain was in the air. Should I close my window? No. I didn't want a stuffy room tonight.

In the summer night, hundreds of frogs croaked and peeped in an off-tune chorus. The yard light always shone into my room unless I pulled the blind down — which I hardly ever did. I didn't like the dark any more. It was comforting to see the pale light outline the hard corners of the packing boxes and draw overlapping window shapes on the slanted gable roof. I turned onto my back and sighed. One good thing — Dad would be gone for almost two days.

I was just dropping off to sleep when I heard something that made my eyes pop open. The frogs' racket had been silenced by a tune played on a harmonica — the same melody that had crept up on me in the fog. This time I recognized the tune. I'd sung it in Girl Guides. "Buffalo Gals, won't you come out tonight, come out tonight, come out tonight? Buffalo Gals, won't you come out tonight, and dance by the light of the moon?" It was a silly song and we'd always sung it loud and fast. But this musician played it slowly, giving it an eerie sadness.

Throwing back the covers, I stepped over cartons, opened the window higher and stuck my head out. Where was it coming from? Ben's room? No. It was definitely coming from Mom's part of the house. Had she taken up playing the harmonica, of all things? She wouldn't have the energy. The guest cabins were way on the other side of the house, behind a thick stand of trees. Maybe it was someone on the veranda. But I'd heard that song this morning, before the guests had arrived.

The music stopped. Nothing moved until a bat flickered from under the stable roof. It disappeared quickly into the murky darkness.

I sat cross-legged on the floor, waiting to see if the strange music would begin again. Before long, my eyes began to droop. Somewhere in the back of my muzzy mind, I thought I heard a sound beside me, as if someone had been listening and was now walking away. Was that the faint clicking of heels on the floor, the swish of fabric sliding against the packing boxes? The bedroom door, glowing mistily white, opened and closed. Or did it? Had I heard it snap shut? Struggle as I might, I was held in that nowhere place between wakefulness and sleep. Only when a cold, damp breeze drifted in the window did I shiver awake long enough to stand up, disoriented and uncertain.

Had Mom been in to check on me? Surely she would have told me to get off the floor and into bed. I shook my head. It felt fuzzy and clogged. I climbed under the covers, searching for a lingering warm spot, trying desperately to sort out what had just happened. Within seconds, however, a gluey darkness closed over me.

The next morning I woke up in a tight bundle under my covers. It was freezing cold and the sheets were clammy. I leaned over to grab a fallen blanket. My fingers touched something warm and hairy. I groped around. And wet. I jumped back with a yelp. Ben's dog, Prue, laughed up at me.

"What are you doing here?" I mumbled sleepily. "Shouldn't you be getting ready for the big ride? And how come you're so wet?"

Prue looked towards the partially open door, then at the window, eyes blinking slowly, pink tongue lolling.

"Looks to me like you've been outside," I said. "I'll bet Silent Sam, your charming owner, is looking for you."

Prue, her gaze locked on the window, whined. I wrapped my comforter around my shoulders and climbed wearily over the pile of boxes to take a look.

A soft shower was flowing down the glass and spraying in. My feet hit an icy puddle. Cursing under my breath I peered out into the yard. When I yanked the window higher, Prue leaped over the boxes to join me.

A line of riders was filing out of the far corral, swathed in dark riding capes, hoods pulled forward. All except the last rider. He wore a short yellow slicker and a black cowboy hat and was leading two riderless horses. Prue trembled and made little whiny sounds. The riders angled towards us along the rail fence. I could hear the squeak of leather, the rustle of plastic, and the low murmur of voices. As they passed by, Prue let out a sharp bark, front paws scrabbling at the ledge.

The rider in yellow looked up. I leaned out and pointed at Prue. Ben shook his head and jabbed a finger in the direction of the lead rider. Then he shrugged. I nodded. Dad, probably in a foul mood because the weather had disobeyed him, had decided to punish someone. Prue was it. Ben lifted one hand in goodbye and before long, the winding line of riders had disappeared into a stand of poplar trees.

"So, Prue," I said, "it's you and me, huh? Winny'll have our heads. But, since we've already missed helping with breakfast, we may as well check on Mom."

Prue sat politely while I dressed, waited outside the bathroom while I washed, and then followed me down the hall towards Mom's room. The original settler, Percy said, had built a small ranch house around the turn of the century, and the next owners had added to it ten or fifteen years later. We were only the third owners. To me, both sides of the house were equally ancient. Still, Winny kept referring to one side of the place as the "old house." The only way you could tell you were going from one part to the other was by the different levels of the floors.

I opened the heavily painted white door. Two steps down and halfway along the hallway of the "old" house, I stopped in front of Mom's bedroom.

This door, painted a dark blue, was shut, as usual. Someone was talking on the other side. Was it Mom? Yes. But she wasn't speaking in her melancholy, forlorn voice — she sounded worked up, excited. Suddenly that tone changed, becoming urgent, pleading. A spasm of dread gripped me. Was she talking to herself? Rambling like a madwoman? Or was someone answering back? The voice or voices were too low to hear clearly.

"This is silly," I muttered. "Probably Winny's in there with her."

I was about to press my ear to the wood when I was distracted by a scratching sound behind me. Prue was backing rapidly away from the door, hackles up, ears flat, eyes rolling.

"Hey! What's the matter with you?" I whispered angrily.

I couldn't deal with two things at once and before I could think twice, I knocked on Mom's door. Silence thrummed through it and sighed up and down the hall, as if the whole house was holding its breath. I waited, then knocked again. It took more than a full minute before the door swung open.

"Mom?" I asked. "Are you okay? I—"

She was wearing her usual flannel nightgown and heavy socks. Black hair floated around her head like a dark cloud, but her face wasn't its usual chalky colour — it was flushed a ruddy pink. Her eyes looked bright and alert, but focusing on me, they became narrow and suspicious — as if she'd been caught doing something she shouldn't and was going to brazen it out.

I took one tentative step into the room. There was no one with her.

"I — I just wondered if you wanted to come downstairs and I'd make us some breakfast," I said. "Then I thought maybe Winny was in here with you — bringing tea or something. I thought I heard you... " My voice trailed off. "... talking to someone."

"Oh... " she said, fingering the collar of her nightgown. "I... I guess I was having a dream... talking in my sleep. I seem to be doing a lot of that since I came here. That's why I moved rooms. I was keeping your dad from getting his rest, he said... that is, Glen said... that he needs his sleep with all this activity going on. Sometimes I have to get up and walk around. I can understand why that would bother him. You run along now. I'm fine. Really. I'm feeling much better."

So, she'd moved rooms because Glen Locke's comfort had been disturbed. It figured.

"I'll be fine now, Jess," Mom repeated. "You run along and help Winny. Go on now, honey." She said it in her sweet voice, but I could feel a desperation growing in her.

Why was she so anxious to get rid of me? To keep her talking, I said, "Did you come into my room last night? To check on me or whatever?"

For a moment she looked surprised, and then uncomfortable, as if she'd just realized something. But she answered in the same soft voice, "No. No, I didn't. I was very tired, Jess. I — look, honey, I'm sorry... I — "

"It doesn't matter," I answered, bristling. "Just curious. No big deal."

She tried to look more cheerful. "Look. You go down and I'll be there in a while. To help. I — I guess Glen and the others have gone?"

"Yeah. I have to leave to meet Ben and him at Webster's Corner with supplies soon. Wanna come? Get out in the fresh air. Just the two of us?"

She shook her head. "You go ahead. I don't want to leave—that is... I don't feel up to it. I'm okay. Really. You can go."

I shrugged away my disappointment. She obviously didn't want to be with me. Fine. If she didn't care, neither would I.

Through stiff lips, I said, "Doesn't matter. I'll take Prue, Ben's dog, with me."

"Ben?" Mom's brow furrowed. She stopped staring around and focused on me.

"Ben," I said, my words clipped. "The boy Percy brought yesterday to help out. Percy's arthritis is acting up. I guess Ben'll be working here for the summer." Something made me lie then, just to see her reaction. "He'll need a room, in this part of the house, Winny says. Maybe he could take the one next to you. You'll have some company."

"No!" she cried. One hand fluttered as if to ward off a slap.

I was instantly sorry. "It's okay, Mom. He can have another room."

"What I mean is," she said, the hand fingering her collar again. "I don't want some strange teenager close by, that's all. He's better off in the other part of the house. What if I call out in my sleep or something? He could walk right in here and frighten me to death. No, I'll talk to Winny. I appreciate her help, but she does make decisions beyond her job. She really does. I'll have to talk to her."

I felt a stab of anger on Winny's behalf. If *she* didn't make decisions, who the heck would? But why waste my breath? "Don't worry. I'll tell Winny," I added brusquely. "You don't have to say anything. She does a great job here, you know. She's done it for years and years."

She nodded fervently. "I know she has. I wasn't being critical. I—it's just that—" Her eyes were darting around, searching again. When she realized I was watching her closely, she turned her back on me and reached for her cigarettes on the little desk. Her hands were shaking so badly that when she finally got one to her lips, she couldn't handle the matches. I took them from her and lit one.

She sucked smoke into her lungs with a gasp, sat down on her wooden rocker and looked out the window. "It's raining. I like rainy days, don't you? Ask Winny to bring me some coffee. I think I'll read in bed for a while. I could hardly put down the mystery I started last night."

I glanced towards the old brass bed. Mom had found a number of ancient quilts and was using them as covers. I didn't see a book on her bedside table or on the bed. Or on the small desk by the window. I felt as if I was seeing her room for the very first time. It was almost stark, with only the bed, her rocker, a desk and an old dresser. Two small woven rugs lay on the dark brown floor.

Her room at home in Winnipeg had always been a mess—clothes and make-up and pretty trinkets every-where. It had smelled spicy, like her favourite perfume. And there had been rows of African violets along the window sills, packed with tiny clusters of pink, mauve or white crystal blossoms. I'd loved that room.

This one made me feel sad and unwelcome. "See you later then, eh?" I said, my voice tight.

Cigarette smoke hung around her head. It was as if she was standing behind a curtain, looking out at me.

"Jess?"

"Yes?"

For just a moment, she looked like she was about to say something—something that made her lean forward, her expression intense, almost frightened. But then she shrugged and turned away to gaze out the window.

Tears burned my eyes. I walked out of the room, dragging the door shut behind me. Prue danced back and forth, her eyes bright, her tail swirling in circles of apology.

"And what got into you?" I snapped.

She bounced around me, as if nothing had happened. Then, she ran a little too far and ended up by Mom's door again. She stood stock-still, her head tilted to one side, listening. With ears back, she slunk past me down the hall. When she reached the white door, she stood with her nose almost touching it, making tiny whimpering noises in her throat. I glanced back at Mom's bedroom door. Prue's pathetic cries grew louder.

"Okay, okay, we're going," I grumbled. "I don't know what's got into you. Or her. You're both acting as if Mom's room's got a spook in there or something."

I stared back down the hallway. What was happening in this house, with its music and its voices and my mother's strange behaviour? I had one answer, but I wouldn't think about it. With grim determination, I opened the hall door and headed for the stairs.

❦❦❦

Willow Creek Ranch, Alberta, 1908, May 12
Sunday evening. I will write down what happened, in the order it happened, or else I will get caught up in ranting about *Her* again, and I have to calm myself first. I was waiting for Father so that we could get on with our latest adventure, *Dr. Jekyll and Mr. Hyde*—a ghastly and

60

wonderful tale by our favourite writer, Robert Louis Stevenson. Quite a difference from *Treasure Island*, but no less exciting. I was sitting by the window when I saw Father emerge from the stable. It had been quite a few days since we'd read together and I hadn't let him know I'd read ahead a little. I could hardly wait to see his face when he realized that Dr. Jekyll and Mr. Hyde were one and the same!

I waved at Father, just to remind him I was still waiting. He looked up at my window, waved, gave a thumbs-up sign and walked towards the house. I made sure our bookmark was placed where it should be and smoothed my hand over the warm leather cover while I waited.

The light dimmed in the room as the evening sun dropped lower and lower behind the dark ring of trees. Where was Father? Why was he taking so long? The answer came with the tapping of heels down the hall.

"Haven't you put on your nightclothes yet?" *She* sighed. "It's past your bedtime, Ian. Come along now."

"I'm waiting for Father," I said coldly.

"I'm afraid he's not coming up tonight," she announced firmly. "He's made an error somewhere in our accounts and it must be sorted out. It seems that your horse has caused even more problems. Your father seems unable to account for the money from its sale. And I can't say that I am impressed by the way things have been going with you either, Ian."

For a moment, I almost smiled. It has been three days since I ruined my algebra problems. Three days of more scraped and ink-blotched pages. Each day, she has returned the same work and each day I have devised new ways of making a mess of it. She thinks that she will break me by making me do it over and over and over again. But I won't give in.

"I'll wait for Father," I announced. "He can't take much longer."

"I assure you, Ian," she answered in a dry voice, "he won't be up tonight."

I stared at her. So this was to be my punishment.

"What is that book?" she demanded.

I gripped it tightly.

"It isn't that hideous rubbish your uncle sent you, is it? I told you to destroy it. Give it to me at once."

I shook my head.

Reaching forward quickly, she snatched it from my hands. When she saw the title, she sniffed, her nostrils flaring as if she'd smelled something disgusting.

"I'll hold on to this. It appears your father has decided to fill your head with this muck in spite of my wishes. Why your uncle bothered to send this all the way from England I have no idea. He should have known better."

She held the book against her chest. "You'll thank me later, Ian. Such fanciful nonsense is not suitable for a boy of your nature."

When her heels had tap-tapped away, I swallowed many times to keep myself from crying out in anger and frustration. Now, as I think about Father downstairs, pouring over the accounts, I find my anger transferring to him. Why doesn't he fight back? Why is he so weak? Why does he allow her to control everything? And now I wonder — dare I go through with the plan that has been formulating in my head?

No. Not yet. Something tells me I'll know when the time is right.

CHAPTER 6

A T TEN-THIRTY, I WAS DRIVING PERCY'S OLD PICK-UP along a winding gravel side road to Webster's Corner. In the back, four battered red tin boxes were lying side by side. Two of them held the camp stove, the cooking gear, and metal plates and cups. In the other two, Winny and I had packed the rest of the food. The rain had stopped, and the wind rushing through the cab was cool and damp. Prue's head hung out the passenger side, her thin body twitching with pleasure.

The hills were quilt squares of hazy green, gold, black and purple. The clouds hung low, blocking out the distant mountains and misting the rolling foothills. I turned on the local country station. We ground our way up and down the rough road to the deep, smooth voice of Randy Travis singing about leaving his woman and feeling real bad about it.

The old truck rattled and shuddered the final few yards up the steep hill. I pulled into a small clearing directly in front of the grey carcass of Webster's Store. A faded sign above one gaping window advertised something called Stubby Root Beer. A couple of rusting gas pumps stood in the grassy yard. The trail that Dad was taking with his guests was about a quarter of a mile behind the old store. They would be setting up camp near Syrup Creek, a sweet, icy stream fed from a high mountain glacier.

Listening to Dolly Parton warble about how she was a wild flower, I sniffed scornfully. Right. Just a wild country rose. Hitch a ride with the wind and take off. That's what *I* should become. A wild flower. Mom used to love Dolly Parton's songs. Would she ever sing along with the radio again, in that funny off-tune voice of hers? Would she ever be well? Or would something inside her finally break into so many pieces that no one could put them together again? Why had I needled her about Ben getting a room in her part of the house? I felt a flush of shame when I remembered the panic in her eyes. I should be helping her; but how do you help someone who seems beyond it?

I tried not to think of that weekend last fall, but as always, whenever I thought about Mom, it slammed into my mind. Scotty hadn't wanted to go on the school camping trip — he'd hated outdoor stuff — and he'd looked so miserable peering out of the car window as Mom and I waved goodbye. Mom hadn't wanted him to go, either.

"Scotty's too withdrawn," Dad had said. "You can't pamper him forever."

"But some kids aren't comfortable camping out with crowds of other kids. It doesn't mean they're missing anything," she'd argued.

"The boy can't spend his entire life with his nose in a book. He should be out playing with others his own age. You've got to let go sometime, Jeanie."

He'd won. And Scotty had gone. And his canoe had tipped over during a flash storm. The kids had been allowed to sit on their life jackets, instead of wearing them. Of the three boys in Scotty's canoe, only one had been able to grab a jacket as they went under. Scotty and the other boy had drowned.

I *hated* thinking about Scotty. I always got this awful panicky feeling that made it hard to breathe. Why did I have to remember the last time I'd yelled at him for losing one of my tapes? Why did I have to remember the way his hair stuck up like a porcupine at the back of his head? Why did I always hear the awful sounds Mom made when they'd told her—the dry gasping screams that went on and on? And then the horrible days of silence that followed. And my anger.

I was mad at her for the silence and the grieving all of these months. Why couldn't she let me have one day—just one lousy day when I didn't have to think about Scotty or about her. I swallowed the pain down. I hated this feeling. I got out of the truck and started hauling at the boxes.

Prue, who'd been snuffling around a rusting gas pump, suddenly barked and ran towards the bush. Into the clearing loped a horse and rider, leading two sway-backed white nags. I felt a rush of relief when I realized Dad wasn't with Ben. Good. I wouldn't have to talk to him right now. Then, just as quickly, resentment took its place. How on earth did my father expect Ben and me to lift those heavy boxes onto the pack horses? Wasn't that just *typical*, I fumed.

Ben tied the horses to an old hitching post and walked over to the truck. A strong wet breeze suddenly blew through the poplars and a big black and white magpie swooped down on it to land in front of us, looking for food. Prue lunged and it took off with a flutter and squawk.

"So, you made it," Ben said, reaching in and grabbing hold of a box.

"Percy showed me the way last week. It isn't *that* hard."

He glanced at me out of the corner of his eye. "Okay, okay. Move over and let me get at these things."

"I'm supposed to help," I said, trying not to snarl. "And where is my father?"

"You can't lift these. Too heavy. Your dad was too busy setting up camp to come."

"And I suppose everyone else was standing around watching?" I asked sarcastically.

"Won't let anyone else help. All those guests eager to give a hand. No dice. Acts like he's got ten arms and no time."

I snorted. "That's my father, all right. But as it's just you and me here right now, I've *got* to help. I'm strong."

He shrugged. "Suit yourself. I'll move the truck over to the horses."

"I can move it," I said, hopping into the cab.

"Suit yourself," I heard him murmur before he walked back to the horses.

I almost laughed out loud when he dragged the first box towards the tailgate and tried to lift it. "Jeez — ooph — what are you feeding these people? Grab the other end. Watch it. It's heavy."

It took us about a half-hour of grunting and groaning and lifting and shoving before we got the leather-strapped boxes fastened to a sort of wooden saddle each horse wore over the heavy pad protecting its back. I spent a good part of the time dancing around the brutes, terrified that one would kick me or step on my toes. I tried to maintain some dignity while ignoring the laughter in Ben's narrow brown eyes.

He spoke only to give me orders. As he seemed to know what he was doing, I followed them. I noticed that the big bruise on the side of his forehead had turned yellow around the edges. He probably got into all sorts of fights. No, that didn't seem likely. Too quiet. Maybe quiet...but deadly. I shook my head and grimaced. My imagination was already working overtime with my mother. I didn't need to think about anyone else's problems.

I watched him fasten the second set of boxes. He towered over me. His hands were square, the fingers short and strong, the wrists thick. Flat muscles strained under the thin blue shirt. Most of the boys I'd known were city kids. Their hands were smooth and young. Ben's hands — tanned, calloused and dirt-grimed — were different. He brushed past me to tie another leather strap, and I felt something inside me sit up — startled and wide awake.

He sorted the horses out, pulled on his yellow slicker and swung up on Bower. Prue wound around Bower's legs, a pleading look in her eyes. I called her and she came reluctantly, her body drooping with misery.

"You stay with her, Prue."

"I have a name, you know. It's Jess."

"More like a boy's name, if you ask me." He pulled Bower's head to one side and moved off, leading the two heavily laden pack horses down a short hill onto the trail below.

"'More like a boy's name if you ask me,'" I mimicked, then shouted, "No need to say thanks! I only sprained a thumb and put my back out! And you can tell my father I hope the cooking tent falls on his head!"

I know he heard me, but he pretended not to. I kicked the nearest tire on the truck and congratulated Jessica Locke on making a complete idiot of herself. Then I shoved Prue into the truck, climbed in, ground the old engine into gear and drove out of the clearing, kicking up gravel.

❦ ❦ ❦

Willow Creek Ranch, Alberta, 1908, May 12
I turned slowly and surveyed the land below me — the
long green valley, the breeze washing deep waves into
the grass and turning the leaves of the trees inside out. I
felt the horse surge forward, its smooth muscles carrying
me up and over the wide crest of the hill. But as we
cleared the crest I saw, to my horror, that there was no
solid ground beyond. The horse's legs stretched down,
down, down. I leaned back in the saddle, using all of my
strength to keep my seat. My cry echoed through the
thick air, returning to me, taunting me. There was
nothing but the blackness of night below. Down, down
we fell.

Just as the horse's rump began to tip slowly, slowly, up
and over my head, I lurched awake, soaked in sweat.
With shaking hands I leaned forward and lit a candle.

Had I cried out in my sleep? As always, the answer
came with the tap, tap, tap of heels down the hall. Would
She never give me any peace?

The door opened. *Why*, just once, couldn't she knock?
I forgot, until it was too late, to blow out the candle.

"What are you doing?" she demanded. She was
carrying a tiny pinch lamp, its short wick casting a dim
light across the floor. The lace of the white nightdress
and her face were lit from below, giving her an unearthly
look. "Are you wasting candles again? Are you reading
instead of resting?"

"I had to use the chamber-pot," I said, through
clenched teeth. The air was chilling my damp nightshirt
and I tried not to shiver.

"What is it, Augusta?" asked a sleepy voice from

down the hall. Father had come out of his room and was shuffling towards us.

"For heaven's sake, Nigel," she snapped. "I can handle the boy. Go back to bed!"

"You okay, old chap?" he called.

"Yes, Father," I answered.

"Righto." He yawned loudly. "Back to sleep everyone, eh? No harm done, eh?"

His door closed, but still *She* remained. A heavy hostile silence dropped between us like a velvet curtain.

"Go away," I said.

I heard the sharp intake of breath.

If she had said nothing and gone back to bed, she might have worn me down in a day or two. But she made a very big mistake.

"I think a lesson in manners might be an appropriate topic for tomorrow morning. A nice *long* lesson on manners, with perhaps an essay. I shall have Madeline take over the household chores for the next few days. I shall be sitting beside you all day, every day, until that work is completed properly. I shall not leave you alone for one second, my boy. Blow out that candle immediately." The door snapped shut and her footsteps receded.

I have no choice now. I must act.

CHAPTER 7

WHEN I DROVE INTO THE YARD, A TOW TRUCK WAS parked by the kitchen door. Leaning against it was one of the biggest men I'd ever seen. His shoulders, massive with humps of bulging muscles, held a broad head with a wide, squared-off chin. He wore filthy coveralls. He took off his greasy cap and ran one catcher's mitt of a hand over a scalp dusty with new growth. I drove slowly past and the man's small eyes followed me. I gave a tentative wave. He didn't move. Looking straight ahead, I aimed the truck for the rutted drive that ran around to the front of the veranda.

Prue woke up with a big yawn when I shut off the engine. The man and his truck were out of sight. I decided to avoid the back door at all costs.

Even before I reached the veranda, I heard shouting from the kitchen. I crept through the dining room and parlour. Prue hid behind a chair, her head down, her ears back. I edged up to the kitchen door.

The man shaking his fist in Percy's face was the same

man I'd just seen at the tow truck. No, he was dressed the same, but he was many years older. He was just as tall, but his head was shiny bald. And it was as if someone had taken a big pin and released the puffed-up muscles of the man outside so the huge bones of his skeleton jutted out from his drooping hide.

Percy leaned towards the massive bony fist and said loudly, "Now, listen to me, Gus Hodge! Ben's old enough to make up his own mind. And smackin' him around won't get you anywhere, either. He could knock you right off your feet if he had a mind to, and you know it."

The big man shook his head. "I never hit the boy—he—"

Percy snorted. "Don't give me that bull. We saw his face. He didn't get that welt walkin' into a wall. His father would be turnin' in his grave—"

The big man bellowed, "Don't you talk to me about his pa! The boy had it comin'. He's to stay at that station and get his work done. Now that summer's come, he's to be helpin' me, not out riding around on that damn horse of his. I have a good mind to get rid of the damn thing. You've filled his head with all sorts of craziness. You—"

"That's just about enough," snapped a voice from behind Percy. For one moment, all that could be heard was the hoarse breathing of the two old men. "Ben's going to be working here this summer," Winny said. "He's old enough to make his own life. He's stuck by you all this time when you didn't deserve it." Her voice lowered. "You've driven him away, Gus. That's what you've done...driven him away. You've punished him long enough. And for something he had nothing to do with. Nothing!"

The terrible old man seemed to stagger back from the words before bellowing even louder than before. Soon, he

71

and Percy and Winny were all shouting at once. And just then, without warning, I was shoved into the kitchen from behind.

"Shut up, shut up, shut up!"

Everyone stopped and stared. At my mother. She was still in her flannel nightgown, her great mop of hair loosed from a braid at the back. Her eyes were wild, her arms pressed hard against her sides.

Winny ran up to her. "It's all right, Missy. He's going. It's all right. Percy, get him out of here!"

Mom pushed her aside and stared at Gus Hodge. "I was trying to... to have some quiet... to... and we — I could hear you upstairs. I heard what Percy just said. About your boy." She took little running steps towards Mr. Hodge. "How dare you, how dare you! Don't you see what you're doing?"

"Who the hell is this?" bellowed Gus Hodge. "You got a crazy woman running the place? Look at her!"

That sobered Mom for a moment. She ran her hands over her hair and down her nightgown and stood up straight, looking the man in the eye. "I am not crazy," she said in a hollow voice. "Sad you don't see what you've done. Saves you the pain of guilt." She frowned as she searched his face. "Who do you think you are? Where do you get the right to do this to your boy? Who gave you that right?" She turned to Winny and her voice became panicky. "Who — who is he? Make him leave. I don't want him in the house."

Gus Hodge took a couple of steps back. "Lady, you're nuts." He turned on Percy. "I'm goin'. But when that boy gets back I'll make sure he don't come here again — or to your place or any other place without my say-so."

Mom stared around at us. "What about the boy? Is he safe?"

I nodded. "Yes, Mom. He's safe. Maybe you should go upstairs now, okay?"

"You runnin' this place for *her*, Percy?" Gus Hodge sneered. "It oughtta last but a few days with an old cripple and a crazy runnin' it."

"Gus! Get outta here. You hear me? Out!" shouted Percy.

"You just remember what I said," snarled Gus Hodge. "And don't think I ain't comin' back for him. 'Cause I am!"

When the door slammed shut behind Gus, Percy bolted it.

Mom's voice caught in her throat. "Don't you see? We weren't much different. We...I am to blame. And now I hear more tears. I feel him there, but he won't talk to me. He's angry with me still. The anger is all around me. That horrible man interfered—just when I was about to ask...I *know* he wants to talk to me. But I...just...can't...*see* him."

Winny led her away, but not before sending Percy a look and nodding towards the phone. Percy dialed and asked for Doctor Ambrose.

"It's an emergency," he said. There was silence for a moment then he spoke again. "It's Percy Eldridge, Steve. Yeah. We need you. Yeah, now. Willow Creek Ranch. What? No. No, Winny's fine. It's Mrs. Locke. The new owner."

I didn't hear the rest. All I could hear was my mother's voice, over and over in my head. What did she mean about more tears? And who wouldn't talk to her? She couldn't see *him*? Who? That awful man had been right. She'd been babbling like a crazy person. Just like this morning when I stood outside her closed door.

Lettice, who'd been hiding in the pantry, slid into the kitchen and the two of us looked out the window. The tow truck was still there. Both men were glowering out the windshield. Then the younger giant leaned forward and the

73

engine kicked over. Backing up, the tow truck circled and slowly drove out of the yard. Two horses, standing at the rails of the paddock, watched it leave before stretching their noses towards the long grass that grew around the fence posts. It all looked so peaceful and ordinary in the shimmery warmth of the early afternoon, but I couldn't stop my teeth from chattering.

Percy ordered Lettice on her way. She grabbed her slicker off the hook on the wall and pulled a tractor cap over her thin braids.

"I knew when I saw that mother of yours that she weren't all there," she said to me in a kindly tone, patting my arm. "I seen her three times now, and each time she has that look about her. Liver. It happens after someone dies, eh? Some of my medicine'll help that liver of hers. My gramma used it when she felt poorly. I'll bring some tomorrow. Don't you worry, Jess, it's just the thing."

Percy growled in her direction. With cheerful mutterings about livers and homemade medicine, she wobbled away on her bike, leaning forward into some imaginary wind.

Percy took my arm and, sitting me down, poured a big cup of hot tea. Then he reached into a cupboard and added a dollop out of a bottle. "Whisky," he said, shoving the mixture at me. "Go on, honey, drink it up."

My teeth clicked against the rim of the cup, but I managed to sip some of the hot liquid. It tasted awful. The fumes went up my nose and into my throat, making me cough.

"Was that—that man really Ben's grandpa?" I gasped.

Percy sat down. "Ben lives with his Grandpa Gus. The young fella waitin' outside was his Uncle Emmet. He lives in a trailer park on the other side of Rosewood."

"Does his grandpa...you know...beat Ben up?"

Percy looked uncomfortable. "Well...Ben and me—I wouldn't want to tell tales behind his back, Jessica. We've known him a few years now. He protects the old man. Watches over him, in a way. Sorry for him. Ben wouldn't like Winny and me to interfere. That's what Ben's like, you see. But we keep an eye on things. The old man drinks. Sorry, Jessica, I—"

I nodded. "It's okay."

We sipped our loaded tea in silence. Warmth was spreading through my body, and my jaw slowly relaxed. I thought about Ben and the swelling on his face and his silent ways, and I understood a bit more. Seeing Percy and that big man scuffling and shouting had upset me, but I knew the real reason for my shakes was Mom. She'd gone over the edge. It had finally happened. I felt sick to my stomach. What would the doctor say about her? Would they have to take her away somewhere?

When Winny walked back into the room, I asked, "Is she okay? Should I go up and see her? What should I do?"

"I've got her tucked up. She seems...I don't know how to explain it...she seems calm now, Jess. On the way upstairs, she was shaking like a leaf, poor little thing, but as soon as she went into that room, she calmed right down. At least, she seemed determined to be calm. I told her we'd call the doctor and she just nodded. I think I'd leave her for a bit, honey." She scowled at Percy. "Don't let that man into this house again. You got anything to say to Attila the Hun, you talk to him outside. Understand?"

"Maybe he won't come back," I offered.

Percy shook his head. "I've known Gus Hodge a long time. He'll be back."

Willow Creek Ranch, Alberta, 1908, May 13

"Ian! Ian Shaw! Open this door at once. Do you hear me? Ian!"

I sat with my back to the desk and gripped my walking sticks tightly in both hands. The morning sun through the window lay like warm hands on my back, soothing me, encouraging me.

"No," I said softly.

"Ian? Where did you find that key? Ian? Open this door at once!"

"No," I said a little more loudly.

"What? What did you say? Are you deliberately whispering so I can't hear?"

"*No*!" I cried. "I'm not opening the door. I want to be alone in my own room. Without you barging in when you feel like it! I'll open it up when I feel like it! And not before. This is *my* room!"

The doorknob rattled noisily, then I heard the heels of her laced shoes clicking away down the hall. I waited. The heels clicked back again and the sound of a key scraped in the lock. I smiled. I had left my key in the lock and had tied it tightly to the doorknob using heavy string. Just to be sure, I shuffled over to the door and held the key in place. It was awful and exciting at the same time. I felt the pressure and movement of her key, but my own — the one I'd found quite by chance on the floor of my wardrobe last winter — held tight.

Unsettled, fearful, yet with an almost wild recklessness, I had finally made a stand, a stand that Jim Hawkins, my hero from *Treasure Island*, would be proud of.

Into the throbbing silence she spoke. I shuddered

when I realized her face was separated from mine by only a few inches of wood.

"I don't know what this is about, Ian," she ground out, her voice thick with anger. "But I won't allow it. We'll see how long you can keep this up. Without food. Today. Or tomorrow."

And with that the heels clicked smartly away.

I put my hand over my mouth. I didn't know whether to crow with laughter or to burst out crying. Was I being bold and daring or had I finally taken leave of my senses?

Now, it is evening and I am more settled. I was prepared, you see. Knowing that I might one day use the key I'd found, I had put away raisins, apples, cheese, biscuits and other bits and pieces to see me through such an event.

The sky darkens. She hasn't been back. I am resolved. I know what I have done and I will face the consequences. There will be consequences. Somehow she'll make me pay.

CHAPTER 8

DOCTOR AMBROSE WAS A SHORT MAN, AROUND MY parents' age, with rusty hair and lots of pale freckles. He spent close to an hour upstairs with Mom. When he came down, Winny sat him at the kitchen table and slid a cup of black coffee and a piece of peach pie in front of him.

He ate the pie in silence, all three of us watching. When he was done, he pushed the plate aside, took a sip of coffee, leaned back and blinked at me through horn-rimmed glasses.

"Well, Jess," he said. "How's the elbow?"

I shrugged. "Pretty good."

"Fine. Fine. Any problems with it, you come and see me. Okay?"

I nodded. He cleared his throat and turned to Winny and Percy. "With Mrs. Locke's husband away, I guess I'd better talk to the two of you. In confidence, of course. Will you be staying the night?"

Percy nodded. "Locke and the others will be back tomorrow sometime."

Doctor Ambrose tapped his lips with one finger and thought for a moment. "I'd like to talk to him as soon as he gets home. Jess, would you prefer not to be in on this? You might want to wait until your father gets back."

I shook my head. In a surprised voice, Winny said, "She's the one who *should* hear this. She's a sensible girl. Looks after her mom. Maybe she'd rather Percy and I weren't here."

"No, no, it's okay. I want you here," I said, my mouth suddenly dry. "Is Mom okay?" I felt as if a bird had flown inside me and was banging his wings against my chest wall.

Doctor Ambrose rummaged around in his pockets and pulled out a pipe and a pouch of tobacco. He filled the pipe, tamped it down and scraped a wooden match across his thumbnail. By the time billows of smoke circled his head, my teeth and hands were clenched tight. I knew what he was going to say. And he said it.

"Your mother needs professional help, Jess. She's been through a nightmare and she hasn't quite woken up yet. Your little brother's death... and then this move that took her away from everything familiar and... comforting. No parent recovers fully from the death of a child, but your mother... well, she's quite lost."

I nodded. "I know."

Watching me closely, he said, "Your little brother Scotty was buried in Winnipeg, your mother tells me. She rambled a bit, but I gather that's where you lived at the time of his death."

"Yes, but—"

He nodded slowly. "She said she couldn't visit his grave any more, because, although she tried every day, she couldn't feel him near her. She couldn't feel his presence in the house, either. She said she used to visit the grave quite

79

often the first few months. I think perhaps your mother feels that Scotty...that Scotty might be angry with her. That's why she agreed to move here. It was so hard to visit the place where he was...uh...placed. And harder not to visit it."

I chewed my bottom lip. "She—she did go quite a lot. To the cemetery. It was only a few blocks from where we lived. I thought it was—well—"

"Weird?" he offered.

I nodded. "Weird...kind of scary. She always seemed lost and empty-looking when she came home. I thought it made her worse, not better."

"Did your father notice these changes?" he asked.

I made a face. "My dad's too busy making a big noise about everything. Mom's not like him. But...well... before Scotty died, she always laughed a lot, you know? And Mom and Dad kidded around all the time. When she got...so quiet, after Scotty died, Dad just didn't seem all that worried. In fact, he was gone most of the time. Setting up the buying of this place, I guess, when he wasn't working overtime. I tried talking to him about Mom, but he just kept saying she'd get better once we got away from Winnipeg. You can see how right he was," I said bitterly.

Doctor Ambrose puffed on his pipe and looked into the smoke for a while. Then he said, "Tell me, Jess, did you bring anything of Scotty's with you?"

"You mean like clothes and things?"

He nodded. I hadn't thought of it before. "No. No, I guess not. Dad gave everything away or threw it out before we moved. He said it wasn't healthy to have stuff around." I added in a quiet voice, "The only thing I kept was Scotty's favourite soccer sweater. He wasn't much of a player, but it was the only sport he liked."

The doctor leaned forward. His bristly eyebrows shot up above his glasses. "I understand your mother is a photographer. Are there pictures of the family around? Of Scotty?"

I tried to remember. "I haven't seen any since we got here. But, there's lots of boxes we haven't unpacked yet."

"I asked your mother if I could see one. She didn't seem to know where to find any," said Doctor Ambrose. He looked as if he was fighting to keep his temper. "I'd like to talk to your father as soon as he gets home. There's the ... the matter of getting some professional help for your mom, among other things. She may need to get away for a while."

My voice caught in my throat. "You ... you — I mean, Mom won't have to be put — to be sent to a ... hospital, will she?" My voice got louder. "She'd never get better! She may be stuck in her room now, but before Scotty died she used to ride her bike or walk all over, looking for places and birds and all sorts of things to photograph. She even has one of a great grey owl and ... and she did tons of us. She took one of Scotty that won a prize. She wouldn't be able to *live* in a place full of crazy people! She — she ... " I could hear my sobbing gasps, grating and loud in the silent room. "You can't!"

Someone put a hand on my back. "No one's going to put your mom away," said Winny. "Isn't that right, Doctor." It wasn't a question. It was a demand.

Funny how, as soon as someone gives you the okay to cry, you can get control of yourself. Percy looked as if someone had taken away his favourite horse. Even his hairpiece was a little off centre. Winny's chin trembled. I tried to smile to reassure her and hiccupped instead. Percy handed me a folded handkerchief and I mopped my face.

"Sorry," I muttered.

"Don't you apologize," Winny said, her voice deep and tremulous. "Other people should apologize for not thinking before they speak." She glared at the doctor.

Doctor Ambrose cleared his throat. "I'm sorry, Jess. Winny's quite right. Look. I have a good friend in Calgary. She's a psychologist who deals with people going through terrible grief. I'm sure she'd be willing to talk with your mother. How about if I contact her?"

I nodded vigorously, unable to speak. He stood up and handed Winny a small bottle of pills.

"Meanwhile, give Mrs. Locke one of these every four hours. If she seems too drowsy, cut them in half. They're a mild tranquillizer and have very few side effects. If there's a problem, call me."

At the door he said to me, "Remember, I want to speak to your father as soon as he arrives home tomorrow." He sounded so cool and professional. But then he smiled. "Call me any time, Jess, okay? You're the one keeping a close watch, so you'll notice if there's any serious change. I won't tell you not to worry, Jess, but most people come out of this just fine."

He pushed through the door, Percy following. When I looked out the window, they were standing by the doctor's car. Percy was doing all the talking. The doctor shook his head, patted Percy's shoulder, climbed into his car and drove away.

I turned and saw that Winny was watching me. She smiled. I tried to smile back, but I was swamped with embarrassment and depression ... and worry. Mom. Telling Dad. Everything. I sat down at the end of the long table and stared at the grooves in the wood. Tears burned into my eyelids. I put the heels of my hands in my eye sockets and rubbed hard.

"You go on up to bed. I'll bring you some supper," Winny gently rumbled. "And then you can read or watch that little T.V. in your room. Okay?"

I nodded and groped my way to my feet. Suddenly I was clasped by strong arms, my ear pressed into the softness of her chest. I patted her back and she patted mine. With one final tight squeeze she let me go. Like a wind-up doll, I followed Prue up the stairs.

❧ ❧ ❧

Willow Creek Ranch, Alberta, 1908, May 14
Last night I dreamed about the boy—my daydream friend. It was the first time he had come into my night-time dreams. When I awoke, it was still dark. I threw the covers back and pulled my bad leg over the edge of the mattress and sat, feet dangling, trying to orient myself.

In my dream, I'd watched a casket dropping slowly into the ground. My friend—the boy with the eager face—was dead. No more would we ride from one adventure to another. Even though it had been difficult to see him in my daydreams lately, I had been so sure that he was—it sounds silly when I say this, but—*alive* somewhere inside my head.

I tried to remind myself that the boy had never been real, I mean to say, a flesh-and-blood person. So he couldn't really die, could he? Surely, I could call him back any quiet evening I wanted. Then why, why did I feel a loss so intense that it made me double up and hold my stomach? And why did I feel such a strong presence in this room? A presence that wept and grieved and ached as I did. Maybe I *have* gone completely around the twist. Mad. I forced myself to stop thinking about the boy. He was just an imaginary friend. He couldn't possibly die. Not unless I chose to have him die.

I was trying to sort out the dreams and the realities of the cold night room when I heard something that made the hair stand up along the back of my bared neck — the swish of clothing sliding along my door, followed by the click and scrape of a key that couldn't open it. Thanks to the complicated method of securing my own key, the door remained securely locked. I trembled, in anger and fear and excitement.

What would *She* have done if she had found the door open?

As it was, I moved cautiously, sliding first one leg and then helping the other under the covers. Very, very quietly, I lay back on the pillows. I was glad I didn't have to use the chamber-pot. It was in the closet with a cover on it. There was a frightful pong off it this afternoon. I'm afraid that small but smelly detail might become a problem if I am to stay much longer in my self-imposed prison. Thinking about the chamber-pot lightened my mood a little and I smiled in the darkness. I should write a story called "The Mystery of the Ponging Chamber-Pot."

Just as I was dropping off to sleep, I felt a cool hand smooth my brow — gentle and soothing. It woke me with a start. A pale woman was leaning over me — a woman dressed in white, with a confusion of dark hair. I could not see her face, but I knew it was not *Her*.

As quickly as she came, she began to move away, drifting and shifting into the blackness until her delicate light was extinguished. Surely I am sleeping, I told myself. But now, as I sit at my desk, writing this all down, I can feel her. She is still here, that gentle presence — even though I can no longer see her. And I know that she is grieving. For whom? For me? For my imaginary friend? What can this mean? I wonder what it is like to lose one's mind. I'm sure it must be worse than this, for this presence is comforting, not frightening. Perhaps she will stay with me for a little while longer — and the sadness and the loneliness will ease.

CHAPTER 9

I DIDN'T REALIZE UNTIL WE WERE ALL CROWDED INTO my little bedroom that Winny had followed Prue and me. She bossed me around, making sure I put on clean pyjamas and washed my face. Then after tucking me into bed, she tried tidying the room, but gave up with a flap of hands and a shake of her head.

"I'll get you something to eat in a bit," she said as she left the room. Within seconds I was asleep.

I was woken up in the yellowy light of early evening by the rattling of dishes. I struggled to a sitting position and Winny carefully placed a tray on my lap—thick minestrone soup, a plate of cheese and fresh bread and a huge glass of milk. I think she was going to stand, hands on hips, until I'd finished everything, but I told her in a thick, drowsy voice that I'd be fine. She humphed, tousled my hair and left.

When Percy arrived to clear the tray away, I smiled at him sleepily, rolled over and sagged into oblivion.

Sometime in the night, I woke up with a start. Prue was sniffing the air and whining, her nails clicking back and forth.

"Prue, lie down!" I snarled.

She began to make throaty growling noises and paced faster. Maybe there was a strange animal in the yard. I snarled again, but she wouldn't give up. Finally, I stumbled out of bed. A drifting splatter of rain rolled lazily down the window. I crouched and peered out towards the paddocks and the line of dark trees. Had Dad and the others come back because of the lousy weather? The light outside the stables reflected mistily in puddles gathering in the empty yard.

I wasn't sure I had really heard it. Please, not again, I begged. But it was there all right, the light notes echoing through the raindrops like tinkling wind chimes. Shivering and getting wetter by the second, I sat hunched by the window, listening to the music fill the air... the room... my head. Then, just as quickly, it was carried away on a small gust of wind and rain.

Across the distant foothills came a faint mutter of thunder. I wanted to get back to bed; I was so tired. But the music sounded as if it had come from the old part of the house. What if Mom had heard it? What if she was lying awake — scared to death?

Dragging myself back over the boxes, I sat on the edge of the bed. The thought of Mom gave me a sickening jolt. I hadn't seen her since that horrible fight in the kitchen. And I was scared to find out for myself what kind of shape she was in. Why was my mind always so jumbled whenever I thought about her? Why couldn't I just handle this in an easy, grown-up way — check on her and then come back to bed? I grunted in disgust. Yeah. Easy.

I fumbled with the bedside lamp. I couldn't find my housecoat, so I pulled a sweatshirt slowly over my pyjama top, puffing with fatigue. Prue sat in front of the closed door staring at me.

"Okay, Prue, out of the way," I mumbled. "You can go outside later, after I've seen Mom. Okay?"

She looked up at me, making funny gulping noises in her throat.

"You really are a dumb dog. Is that all you ever do? Whine and whimper? Whimper and whine and run away and hide?" I grumbled, reaching for the door handle. Prue growled deep in her throat, trembling from head to tail.

Maybe she was sick. I touched her nose. It was cold and wet. She closed her mouth over my hand, tugging gently. Her message was clear: go back to bed.

That pulled me out of my lethargy long enough to snarl back at her, "Prue! Stop it. Now get out of the way. Go on!"

She shifted reluctantly to one side and slid on her belly right under the bed. Only her tail stretched dolefully from beneath the hiding place. I looked longingly at my tumbled bed, but something told me I had to see Mom.

When I opened the door, a wall of sooty blackness almost stopped me. I'd forgotten about the burned-out bulb in the hall ceiling. I stumbled along, guiding myself with hand on cold plaster. When I reached the bathroom, I leaned in and turned on the light. My shadow, huge and distorted, led the way down the rest of the hall.

I hesitated when I reached the white door that led into Mom's hallway. Did this part of the upstairs have an overhead light? Logic said there must be one, so I opened the white door a crack and reached into the cool air behind, feeling the wall.

Nothing. Great.

Edging through the door, I peered around. A window at the end of the short hall offered just enough light to make the scene appear strangely warped. The hall seemed longer and narrower, and the shadows along the length of the baseboards were as dense as black soil. I stepped forward, the boards smooth and icy cold under my bare feet.

I wrinkled my nose. Mould and damp and something else — something sweet and aged, the dense aroma of dusty flowers — hung in the air. I sneezed. Just as I blinked, about to sneeze again, something at the end of the hall moved, as if a shadow had been torn away from the wall. The urge to sneeze died away. At the same time, a freezing flow of air rushed along the narrow space, raising goose bumps all over me. The shadowy shape at the end of the hall grew into a dark low mass and floated slowly towards me. The door clicked shut and I groped for the handle, staring in dread at the thing that moved along with the velvet blackness — a long thin line that undulated and flickered and glowed, like a strip of neon lighting.

When the thin edge of light stopped at Mom's doorway, the black clot of shadow spread across the floor and the line began to change shape. It was as if a paper cut-out, held on edge, was being turned to show me its full flat side. A woman? It had the shape of a woman — wearing a long nightgown or loose dress. Its hair — a shimmery glow of pure white — was knotted high on the head. At the neck was a pile of what could only be lace — frothing white lace on a white, white dress. Why couldn't I see her — *its* — face or hands? They were part of the surrounding blackness.

The white hair leaned close to Mom's door, as if an unseen ear was listening intently. Could it be Mom? Dressed in some weird get-up? Had she found some old clothes and a wig and taken to wandering aimlessly up and down the hall?

I cleared my throat. "M-Mom? Is that you?"

My voice echoed along the corridor. The figure

straightened and the glowing head turned. I sucked in a painful breath. Except for the greyish outline of a long nose and arched brow, the face was black. Where the eyes should be, two small points of light hung in the darkness. Whether those glowing dots could see me or not, I didn't know, but I cried out to my mother again — this time for help.

Like a strong wind down an air shaft, a high-pitched answer roared around me, a sound like the one Mom made when she heard about Scotty's death — grief and fear and pain mixed together. The scream spun through my head, making me horribly dizzy. Was I drifting backwards? I lost all sense of where I was until suddenly the floor rose up and banged into me.

When I opened my eyes, it was still night. I tried to move. My chipped elbow was skinned and throbbing and my hip hurt. I'd fallen hard. I sat up, very slowly. What had happened? Obviously, I'd fainted. Sleepwalking? I'd sleepwalked as a kid and a few times after Scotty died.

But surely I'd been awake, from the moment I sat up in bed tonight — turning on the bathroom light, searching for the hall switch, watching the shadow darken and move. I rubbed my elbow, my hip, my head. It hurt to move. To think.

Was it possible that Mom's terrible sadness had taken on a life of its own? Wandering around the house — listening outside the room, waiting for her to wake up so that it could enter her thin body again? I shook my head. Ooph. Still dizzy! I'd better watch it, or I'd end up chasing even more dark illusions around the hallways.

I stood up inch by inch, afraid to touch the walls. Something was different. The smells and the coldness were gone. I dared to look around. Soft moonlight cloaked the hall, and the shadows had lightened into perfectly ordinary shadows. Best of all, there was no weird figure looking like ... like the negative of a photo. That was it! That's what she'd looked like! That's why I hadn't been able to see her face and hands.

I rubbed my aching hip and muttered, "Sleepwalking. That's all it was. Sleepwalking." Somehow the fall had woken me up from a bizarre dream. I had to believe that.

I turned to go back to my room, then hesitated. What about Mom? I had to check on her. I crept up to her door. Imitating the figure in white, I leaned forward and listened. Whispering. Hushed, urgent whispering on the other side of the door. Two people? Or one? Gritting my teeth, I reached out and turned the door handle.

ੴ ੴ ੴ

Willow Creek Ranch, Alberta, 1908, May 14
It is now evening—the end of my second day. For the first time in my life, I heard my parents arguing loudly. Their voices came from down the hall. They must have been in *Her* room, for Father's room is next door to mine and the voices would have carried better.

Pressing my ear against the panelled wood, I heard Father shout, "Keeping him locked up like a prisoner and now he's locked you out! Augusta, think about what you're doing."

"He's got to get into a good school. In England. It's the only way he'll survive," she cried. "We've got to prepare him, he's got to work hard!"

"We can prepare him, but let the boy have some enjoyment," exclaimed Father. "What harm would there be in his having a horse of his own? You can't—"

Their voices faded. Carefully, I turned the key and eased my door open a crack.

"I've warned you, Nigel. I must have control of Ian. If you fight me on this, I'll go back to my father and take him with me." Her voice was hard and cold.

To my amazement, Father's matched hers. "I'm sick of your threats. Do you hear me, Augusta? And don't get that look on your face. He's *my* son, too. He's old enough to make up his own mind! Look at him, holed up in his room like a frightened rabbit. And don't talk to me about running home. I know you, Augusta. You wouldn't go back to your father without your husband."

"I'd say I was on holiday," she said defiantly.

"And I'd make sure certain people knew you had left me!"

"And how would you do that?" she asked, mocking him. "Write everyone letters?"

"I'd come and demand him back!"

The anger in Father's voice astounded me, but the silence that followed was truly frightening. I shut the door quietly and locked it.

CHAPTER 10

I PEERED INTO THE MURKY ROOM AND COULD HAVE
sworn I saw movement by the window, but then it was
gone. The whispering stopped. A rocker stood a few
feet from the desk, outlined by dusky light from the
window. It was slowly rocking.

"M-Mom?" My voice trembled.

"Jess? Is that you?"

Gripping the door jamb, I dragged in two or three big
gulps of air. The room seemed to tilt for a moment, then
stabilized. "Yeah, yeah, it's me."

An arm reached out from the rocker towards the desk. A
scratch and then a small flame. Her face aglow in the
golden light, Mom touched the wick of a candle with the
match.

"Are—are you okay?" I asked.

She was wearing a nightgown and over that, a fringed
shawl. Her hair was pulled back into a high ponytail,
candlelight accentuating the hollows of her eyes and
cheeks. I was reminded of the strangely lit figure in the hall.
The figure I'd *dreamed*, I reminded myself.

"Jess. I'm glad you came tonight." She seemed to be picking her words carefully. "I was thinking about you." She stretched out one hand.

I walked forward and held it, cold and very light, in mine.

"I've made a decision. I have to tell someone," she said. "I hope that you'll accept what I'm about to say. You know...just...listen. You're all I have now."

Dad. I knew what she meant.

She withdrew her hand. "Sometimes...sometimes, I think I've lost control of my mind," she said in a thin, but curiously matter-of-fact voice. "And other times I know that he is quite real. That he is, in fact, here."

My legs were so wobbly, I kneeled down on the floor. A cold sweat gathered on my back.

She was looking at her hands, the fingers locked. "He won't—*can't* talk to me. Perhaps he doesn't know how. But I hear his music. Remember how he loved his flute? Tonight I heard it. It didn't sound like a flute—more like a harmonica, but it must have been distorted somehow. I wasn't able to get a good look at it. Just a flicker of silver."

This was nuts. I'd heard that music.

My silence made her glance up. She must have read the confusion in my face, because she shook her head. "I guess he's always been with me. But I couldn't feel him, you know? But now—now he's beginning to show himself. I'm just catching glimpses of him. His hair. His hands. I didn't know what was happening at first and I was afraid I was losing my mind. But yesterday afternoon, I saw his, well... his outline—sitting at this desk, writing—and...oh, Jess...he was crying. I've heard his crying every day since I got here. At first, I thought it was a woman, but then I knew it was a boy. His...the sounds are all around me."

Her hands pulled and plucked at her nightgown. "And then...tonight...when the music began, I saw him again—bits of him, like shreds of coloured silk floating around me. He was lying on the bed. And...and this time, I'm sure he saw me!"

I tried to keep my voice steady. "Who, Mom? Who saw you?"

Her eyes were puzzled. "Don't you understand? It's Scotty! It has to be Scotty." Her voice rose. "He's found me at last!" Two bright patches of colour appeared on her cheeks.

"M-Mom. It can't be," I whispered. "Scotty's dead."

She stood up, almost knocking me over. I remained kneeling, watching her pace back and forth. "Of course he's...he's gone. I know that. But don't you see? I couldn't feel him around me before. And now I can! The straight brown hair. The thin pale arms. If only I could see his face. I can't see his face."

"Mom. Please. Sit down," I whispered. "You're scaring me."

"Don't be afraid, Jess. I'm not—I'm just upset because I don't know why he's crying."

"Mom—this can't be—"

She ignored me. "But then...but then I feel something else from him. An anger...frustration. And a deep, deep hurt. Sometimes these feelings are in the room with me and sometimes I can feel them coming at me through the door like a cold dark wind." She shivered. "At times, I'm almost certain there's someone else with him. I don't know how or who...but I can feel her."

Her? The floor shifted under my knees. I closed my eyes for a moment, and when I opened them, Mom's face was inches from mine. I could smell her body odour, dense and heavy.

"I'm sure it's a her," she whispered. "Once, I saw the flick of a long skirt, but I told myself I was just imagining it. Imagining her. And him. That I was overtired. But things kept happening." She gripped my arm, and kneeled down beside me. "I know Scotty is here. But why is he so angry? How can I help him? And who is *she*?"

That's what was worrying her? She wasn't worried about seeing things that couldn't possibly be there? She had completely flipped her lid, and *that* didn't bother her? I would have laughed, but she was scaring me to death.

"I know I let him down, Jess. I was so busy preparing my photographs for that stupid book that will never get published. And I let your dad talk me into sending Scotty on that camping trip. That must be it! Scotty hasn't forgiven me. Do you think that's it?"

I grabbed her arm and spoke slowly, as if to a frightened child. "Mom, he would never be mad at you. It was a terrible accident. You didn't cause his canoe to tip over."

"But he's trying so hard for me to see him. He keeps fading away." Her face crumpled, but she didn't cry. I wondered if she'd ever cry. "Oh, Jess. I haven't been able to feel Scotty near me since he died. I thought leaving Winnipeg would make the emptiness go away. But...since we've arrived here, so many miles away...I started worrying...afraid that Scotty wouldn't be able to find me. He wouldn't know where I'd gone. I think...I'm sure he's found me. There I was wishing for him to be near me and now I wish he hadn't come back. That he was...you know...at peace."

She was crazy. Really crazy. I stood up. It was my turn to pace around the room. A sick anger swelled up in me. Before I could stop it, it burst out.

"Mom! Look at me. Look at me! Scotty is not here. Scotty is *dead*. He has not searched for you. He *is* at peace or whatever you call it. He's *gone*! You're either imagining him or you're dreaming him. It can happen to anyone.

"What you've gotta do is figure out what's real and what isn't! Don't you see? Look..." I hesitated, "...well, I—I had something happen tonight that seemed real—but it wasn't. I haven't sleepwalked in ages. But here I was, standing out in your hall and—" I snapped my mouth shut and took a deep breath. "You're probably dreaming—or sleepwalking, like I was."

"What did you see in the hall?"

I couldn't answer. What had she seen? What had I seen? Was it Mom standing at her own door? Was it—? No! Now I was thinking crazy. I wouldn't—couldn't tell Mom. It would only feed into her craziness. I had to get her to bed and call the doctor in the morning.

"Jess, what—?"

"I was just dreaming," I said quickly, flapping one hand in the air. "Did—uh—did you take those pills the doctor left?"

She shook her head. She looked so small kneeling there on the floor. I felt as if I was *her* mother.

"Winny left me one," she said haltingly, "but I didn't take it. It's still on my bedside table. Jess, you think I'm just imagining all this, don't you? I don't blame you."

I put my hand on her shoulder. "Maybe you should take the pill and get a decent rest, huh? A few hours' deep sleep. We can talk about this again. In the morning, okay?" I sounded like a night nurse in an old folks' home. But it seemed to work.

Not looking at me, she nodded and allowed me to help

her up. She felt weightless, bones as narrow and delicate as a bird. She slid under the covers, swallowed the pill with some water, and lay back on the pile of pillows.

"Don't leave yet," she said, in a small voice. "It's not that I'm afraid of Scotty. I'm not. I just, you know... I just want someone — who's real and... you know."

I nodded.

Her eyes roamed the room, as if looking for something. "I just wanted to know that Scotty was okay. And now — now I can feel him. He's so unhappy, Jess. It hurts me to feel his pain." She put fingertips to her breastbone.

What about my pain, I wanted to cry. Don't you feel *my* pain? "I know," I said, swallowing the bitterness down.

She took my hand and squeezed tight. Searching my face, she said, "I know I can't *tell* what's real and what isn't. And yet I'm so sure I'm seeing and hearing these things when they happen. Do you think I'm — that I've ...?"

I hated to lie, but it seemed the right thing to do. "I think your mind is tired. You're strung out, that's all. You need to get up and around. Talk to Winny and me more... and Dad."

For the first time that night she smiled. "Talk to Dad. About missing tack and next month's feed bill? That's all *he's* willing to talk about."

My voice hardened. "At least you'll know you're worrying about something real. Maybe that's exactly what you need."

She murmured irritably, "What I need, huh? Are you so sure of what I need?"

"I'm not sure of anything," I snapped. "But it's worth a try, isn't it?" I couldn't go on. Her eyes were dimming. "I'm sorry, Mom," I whispered.

Suddenly, clutching my hand, her voice became eager. "I

can prove I'm not seeing things. He'll be back. I'm sure of it, Jess. And if you could be here when he comes, you'd see him, too. Would you try? Maybe you can understand what he wants."

I closed my eyes and nodded, my heart sagging like a lump of wet clay. A voice inside me finally said it: the hospital. How else would she get away from imaginary people in a wide-awake nightmare? When I opened my eyes and glanced down, she was asleep. The pill had worked quickly. Above the sweep of dark lashes, her eyelids were pale and paper thin. Was this really the person who'd shown up at every single parents' day at school, taught me photography, and baked sixteen lopsided birthday cakes over the years, just for me — each one more gaudy and candle-studded than the last?

I tucked her hand under the covers, stumbled down the hallways to my room and fell on my bed. Only then did I cry at the hopelessness of it all.

❧ ❧ ❧

Willow Creek Ranch, Alberta, 1908, May 15
I finally turned the key and opened the door. Day three. Not very long for a heroic stand, I know. But this morning Father knocked gently on my door.

"Ian, dear chap," he said, "I wonder if I might talk with you a moment."

I hesitated. He knocked again.

"She's not here," he said. "She's downstairs. Could we have a bit of a chat, Ian? Just you and me?"

"What about?" I said, my voice high in my throat. "I heard you arguing. Is it about that?"

"In a way," he said. "She told me all about the

arithmetic problems and the book. We've — er — talked. I can't say she's seen the light where you are concerned, but she *is* willing to overlook this — er — this rather unfortunate locked door business — if you agree to do your work properly from now on. You see?"

I sighed. And when I spoke, I heard the stubbornness in my words. "Obey, obey, obey. I can't, Father. I've had enough."

"Look, may I come in, dear boy? Just to talk. I promise I'll go and you can lock up the room again if I haven't given you reason to keep it open."

I stared at my fingers, trying to think. Then I made my way to the door. With one hand on the key, I asked, "Do you promise?"

My father's voice was solemn. "Yes. I absolutely swear."

I opened the door. He stepped into the room, closed the door and twisted the key in the lock. Then, hands in his pockets, he looked at me and smiled. "Might stay in here with you a day or two, myself. What do you think?"

I could feel a smile tugging at one side of my mouth. "You're welcome to join me, Father, but I'm afraid I've only one chunk of very stale bread and a handful of dried apples left."

He nodded. "Aah, well. It was a nice thought." Then his nose wrinkled.

"It's in the closet," I said grimly. "Awful, isn't it? Would have driven me out today or tomorrow, I'm afraid."

We both laughed softly.

Sitting down on the edge of my bed, he looked at me closely. "What have we done to you, old boy, eh? We've been bloody awful parents, haven't we?"

He looked so hurt that I said, "Well, *you* haven't, Father. *You* tried, at least."

That made him look even sadder.

"Not nearly hard enough, I'm afraid. I've always taken the easy road where she's concerned." He sat up straighter and his eyes gleamed. "She's off to a lying-in today. Dennis Gallagher drove over just now. Mrs. Gallagher, as you may remember, has had difficult—er—confinements. This time Gallagher is taking no chances. He's come a week or so ahead of time."

I could feel my whole face brighten. "She's leaving? Now? For a fortnight?"

He nodded. "Of course, Mrs. Gallagher might have the child sooner. But your mother will be away a week at least, I should think. She wanted to take you with her."

My chest tightened. "No! I—"

Father cut me off. "She *wanted* to take you with her, but I think I've persuaded her that she needs this time on her own. She hasn't been away from the ranch for months."

I felt a rush of relief. "Then I'll be staying here, Father. With you."

"She's not entirely convinced yet, old chap. You'll have to promise her to work hard at the school work she'll leave you. You'll have to promise me, too."

"Yes, yes, Father. I promise," I cried, clasping my hands tightly.

I agreed not to lock the door. He left, taking the chamber-pot with him.

A few minutes later, *She* came up and put a covered tray on the desk where I was working. She said nothing about my school work, which I was already bent over, carefully marking out my problems. She said nothing about the key. I wouldn't have given it to her, even if she'd asked. I had hidden it again by tying it to a piece of string and dropping it down the same slot I keep this journal in. Something in my face, when our eyes briefly held, must have told her not to demand it. Her silence was more meaningful than any words she might have spoken. I could see it in the tightened lips and the steely glint in her eyes.

Will she change her mind at the last minute and force me to leave with her? I can hear her coming! I must go.

CHAPTER 11

I WOKE LATE, FEELING AS IF SOMEONE HAD USED AN acetylene torch on my eyelids. When I groaned aloud, the mattress bounced a couple of times and a sharp nose poked out from under the bed.

"You chicken feather, Prue. I should have listened to you last night and stayed in bed." I rubbed my aching scalp with the tips of my fingers.

I staggered to the bathroom for a couple of coated aspirins. There was a huge bruise on my right hip. I'd never hurt myself sleepwalking before. I made the shower water as hot as I could stand and let it run down my suffering body.

Two things kept rolling around in my head and bumping into each other. What was Mom seeing in her room? And had I really seen that black and white figure—I mean, *actually* seen it? Sometimes I remembered vague bits of my previous sleepwalking adventures, but they were always pretty dull. Dad or Mom usually told me the details of what I'd said or done. Why should I remember *this* one so clearly?

I towelled dry, feeling an urgency to see Mom, but afraid to. It was already eleven o'clock. No doubt Winny and Percy had been in the house for hours. First I'd check that Mom was okay and then I'd tell Winny what had happened during the night. Maybe she'd have an opinion on Mom's mental state. I zipped my jeans, pulled on a T-shirt and stared at my dim reflection in the misty mirror. I wasn't even sure *I* was real any more. Did that narrow face, the black curly hair and those dark shadowy eyes belong to me? Or was I living in someone else's dream? I shook my head and water droplets fanned across the mirror. No! If I started asking questions like that, I'd go nuts.

Five minutes later, I was licking toothpaste off my lips, facing the white door into the old part of the house. What could I say to her? What condition would she be in? And what would happen when the doctor talked to Dad later today? Maybe now he'd listen to someone. Maybe I could stop worrying about her. I made a face. Dad listen? Me stop worrying? Never.

I pushed through the white door and walked briskly down the hall, followed by Prue, who was happily snuffling in corners. I rapped sharply on Mom's door.

"Mom?" I said loudly. "It's me. Can I come in?"

No answer. I knocked again. Nothing.

Now what? I turned the handle and stuck my head around the door. Her bed was unmade. The room was empty and smelled of stale smoke.

I sat down in her rocker to wait. Wait for what? For Mom to appear like one of her ghosts? Maybe she'd gone to get some tea. I'd hang around for five minutes, then go looking. I didn't want to face her and Winny together until I'd had a chance to talk to Winny first.

The ashtray on the little desk was overflowing with butts.

She must have been up early and sat here smoking, because there had been only a few butts in the ashtray last night. Wrinkling my nose at the dank smell, I opened the window and sat down again in the rocker, my back to the light. Slowly I began to rock. My muscles slackened and my eyes drooped. The pillow tied onto the back of the wooden rocker felt warm and soft. Allowing myself to enjoy the breeze that lifted my hair and wafted lightly over my arms, I let my thoughts drift away. In the distance, I heard the quick clicking of Prue's nails. Muzzily, I wondered why she was leaving but didn't really care. I was floating on a feathery cloud.

I came to with the sort of jolt you get when you miss a step that isn't there. My eyes snapped open and my heart leaped into action. I knew without looking that someone was behind me. Near the bed. Watching.

A slow buzz of electricity travelled from my sneakers to the tips of my hair. Slowly, slowly, I turned and edged my face past the back of the rocker. Just in front of the bed, flickering bits of colour danced up and down like dust motes in sunlight. Suddenly, they grew larger and brighter.

What could be causing this? Was there a crystal hanging somewhere in the room, scattering light at that one spot? I looked around but saw nothing. Reluctantly returning my gaze, I saw the brilliant scraps of colour begin to merge and solidify, taking on a human shape in front of my eyes.

I leaped to my feet and, without looking back, skimmed across the floor, flung open the bedroom door and ran downstairs.

"Winny!"

"In the larder!" a voice boomed back. Winny's head appeared around the storage cupboard door. "So. You're finally mobile. What's up?"

I stared, not believing she was in front of me, solid and alive and recognizable.

"You okay, Jess?" she asked, her smile changing to concern.

"Where's Mom?" I gasped. "I—I can't find her."

Winny pushed the larder door shut with one foot. She pulled on one of the deep drawers under the counter and tipped the sugar sack she held in her arms. A stream of white granules fell into the tin-lined bin below.

"You're not going to believe this," she said slowly, "but that mother of yours came down about an hour ago, dressed in jeans and a sweater. Took a tin cup of coffee and told me she was going for a long walk. Could have knocked me down with one push of her little finger. She had her watch on, said she'd be here in time for lunch. I told her the guests would be back around four or so. Just to warn her. But she smiled sweetly and said she would be back well before then. She looked pretty shaky but in control, Jess. Maybe those pills are already helping, eh?"

Gaping at her, I said, "But... will she be okay?" I had visions of her jumping off a cliff or something.

Winny nodded thoughtfully. "I think she'll be just fine. Come on, eat some breakfast."

Reluctantly I sat down and stared at the warmed eggs Winny put in front of me. Scrambled. With cheese. The sight of them made me sick.

Why did Mom go for a walk this morning? Had she also seen that thing made up of scattered lights and made a run for it? Was she seeing things that came from her own mind? Or was she seeing something else—something that was *there*, but...well...*not* there. Like I'd just seen. Could it be...I could hardly say it...would those strange scraps of colour have turned into my little brother? No. I couldn't believe that Scotty was in that room with me. I had dozed off in the rocking chair. It had to be another dream.

"You don't want anything to eat?" Winny asked. "You'll end up like your mother. Skin and bones. If she ate properly, she'd be in better shape. I don't want you going down that road."

"Huh? No...I—I just don't feel like eating."

She felt my head. "Well, you're not hot. Probably just a backlash from yesterday. Anything else happen that you want to talk about?"

I looked up into her honest face and chewed at my bottom lip. "No. No, nothing. I'm just—well—kinda tired—wiped out, that's all."

"How about if I give you a nice quiet job to do?"

"Like what?"

"Like going up into that room next to your mom's, the one overlooking the veranda, and sorting through the stuff in it. Mary Parks' son, Walter, is coming over sometime next week to pick up the things his mother left behind when she moved into that seniors' home. He was supposed to pick everything up weeks before you moved in. Now he's decided he wants it. Typical. We dumped a lot of your cartons in with Mary's stuff. I'd like you to separate everything into two piles. Yours and the Parkses'. Could you do that? It might take a day or two."

I shrugged. "Sure, I guess."

"Take a couple of felt markers and mark which are which. That would be a big help. Maybe Ben can lift the heavy cartons when he gets back."

"I'll see how I do," I said, hoping I could manage the boxes on my own.

If I took the front stairs, I could avoid walking past Mom's room. Somehow I couldn't imagine a ghost appearing amongst boxes labelled Safe Move Van Lines.

"I wasn't going to let anyone have these until later," Winny said, lifting a big black pan out of the oven. I realized the air was full of the smells of cinnamon and yeast. "But maybe I can get that appetite of yours kick-started, eh?"

She set the tray on the counter, pulled off a big, coiled cinnamon bun and plopped it on a plate.

"Here. Take it upstairs with you. Let it cool a bit. But don't come downstairs without it inside you. Got it?"

I took the plate, muttering about bossy old women. She gave me a flat-handed push on the shoulder and then grabbed me and hugged me hard. I walked up the front staircase with a stupid grin on my face.

The room was jam-packed with junk. Not just boxes, but old mattresses, headboards, shadeless lamps and piles of ancient pillows and rough blankets spilling out of ripped or sagging cardboard cartons. Raising the blinds that covered the two windows, I almost choked on the dust. Sunlight streamed through the dancing particles.

Sitting on a stack of boxes, I picked at the cinnamon bun. It was soft and sweet. Bit by bit it disappeared. I licked my fingers until all trace of the syrupy maple flavour was gone.

I contemplated the mess in front of me. Many of the cartons were ours, but over in the far corner there was a teetering pile of unmarked boxes heaped on what looked like an old rollaway bed lying on its side. The cardboard was dark and grungy, some of it water-damaged. The boxes looked fairly small. I could move them into the hall, making it easier for Mr. Parks to collect them.

Some of them smelled musty and unpleasant, but it was when I was lifting a crumbling hatbox that I noticed a different odour. Someone had written "The Shaws, 1903–1908" across the peeling, silvery lid with a thick black pencil. Mary and Bill Parks were the people Winny and Percy had worked for. Who on earth were the Shaws?

The lid of the hatbox was broken and when I shifted my hands, it slid to the floor, landing at my feet. The smell from inside the box became almost overpowering—the very same odour, like an ancient potpourri, that I'd picked up last night in the hallway outside Mom's door.

My eye was caught by a rectangle of shiny blackness lying on top of some yellowed pages. It was as if someone was behind me, urging me to take the thing in my hand. Anxious perspiration gathered at the back of my neck and under my arms.

This was silly. It was only the large negative of a photograph, an ordinary everyday object. Then why did the house seem to breathe and shift, as if filled with a new and different energy? Maybe this house—maybe there was someone in this house who wanted me to...what? Supporting the box with one arm, I picked up the old negative and held it to the light.

On the sooty piece of film were the pale shapes of the face and upper body of a woman—the old-fashioned hairdo and high-collared dress, both a whitish grey—the one visible hand a clotted black. But the angle of the light that shadowed part of the face accentuated the other—a narrow straight nose, high cheekbone, and one rather long hooded eyelid under a beautifully arched eyebrow. The eyes were white dots, surrounded by shadows. I choked back a cry.

It was the woman from the hall.

I dropped the hatbox and the negative and ran. Flinging

the door open, I pitched myself down the stairs, out the veranda and along the gravel road. I ran and I ran until I was doubled over with side-stiches. You have to think calmly and rationally, I told myself fiercely, arms wrapped tightly across my chest. You can't just bolt whenever anything strange happens. Finally, when the stitches loosened, I began the slow walk home.

As I approached the wide clearing, the ranch buildings and corrals looked different. I stood by the fence and gazed around. The buildings stood in an unearthly shimmering light. The trees were smaller. The trim on the house was a different colour—a dull reddish brown—and the newer addition was missing. I knew I was seeing everything as it had once been. Gradually, the light dimmed and the rest of the house wavered into view, along with Percy's blue pickup.

My heart beat heavy in my throat. Something was happening in that old place. Something strange and awful and impossible. Something from the past—of that, I was certain. What Mom had to do with all of it, I didn't know. No running away this time. I had to find out what was happening. On my own.

Suddenly, I realized something—maybe Mom wasn't crazy after all. If she was seeing these strange things, she could be confusing them with Scotty. I'd have to keep my mouth shut for now, at least until I'd figured out why the past had suddenly moved forward in time.

If it meant searching through that hatbox for more information, I'd do it. Only this time, I'd take someone with me. Even Ben. With him there, I wouldn't be afraid. Besides, it would take guts to stay in the same room with the silent Ben Hodge. Bravery, I decided, came in different shapes and colours.

❦ ❦ ❦

Willow Creek Ranch, Alberta, 1908, May 15
I stood at my upstairs window, my walking sticks gripped in both hands. As *She* walked towards Mr. Gallagher's wagon, I was sure that my heart had actually stopped beating. Would she change her mind at the last minute?

An hour earlier, she had been in my room, checking the pages I'd finished. She had nodded with satisfaction at the neat order of the numbers and had made me promise that I would finish all the work she had left for me.

"Otherwise..." she said in her clipped voice, "otherwise, you will not be allowed the privilege of remaining behind next time. I hope you don't play the fool again."

I almost smiled. But instead, I hung my head and muttered something that seemed sincere, even to my ears.

"Your father has made me a promise, too," she continued. "If he fails to keep it, he knows that I will ensure that you are never under his influence again."

I didn't know what she meant. I vowed to find out what Father had promised in order that I could be left at the ranch. Did she intend that I find out from him? I looked up. She was watching me intently, but something in her eyes told me she was pleased.

She thinks she's won, I thought. She's found a new way to blackmail us. When she left my room, I sat for a long time, thinking.

Watching her walk across the yard, I wondered how the small feather in her town hat had the temerity to flutter in the breeze. The coil of hair at the nape of her neck shone with tautness. Her back, in its buttoned waistcoat, was as straight as a fire poker.

She refused Father's hand and looked to Mr. Gallagher for help onto the wagon. Once seated, she gestured for her carpet-bag to be hoisted behind her. I bit my lip. It still wasn't too late for her to change her mind.

Mr. Gallagher climbed aboard and raised a hand in goodbye to Father. Only then did I feel the tightly wound knot inside me begin to loosen. She looked up at the window and it contracted again. When I raised one hand, I was surprised to see that it was trembling. She did not acknowledge the gesture. Nor did she respond to Father's few words. Instead, she looked straight ahead and continued to do so as the wagon slowly disappeared around the sharp bend of the road.

I slumped into my chair, sick with dizziness and relief.

CHAPTER 12

I ALMOST EXPECTED THE KITCHEN TO BE DIFFERENT, FULL of strange furniture and different cupboards. But there was Winny, standing at the big wooden table, slicing ham.

"Mom home yet?"

She shook her head. "No. Not yet. It hasn't been that long. Don't worry." But she looked worried.

Lettice was sitting on a stool, cutting and buttering cinnamon buns. She reached under a shelf, pulled out a paper bag, thumped it on the wooden countertop and ripped off the paper. Inside was a corked pop bottle filled with a thick greenish liquid.

"I brung some of my liver tonic for your mom, Jess."

Winny swiped the bottle and pushed it deep into a nearby cupboard. "We'll just put it there to keep it safe," she rumbled and winked at me.

"I'm through upstairs, for now," I said, not wanting to leave Winny's side. "Anything I can do here?"

"Well, let's see. You can help make sandwiches for the guests."

I grabbed a stool and we buttered and slapped ham or chicken salad between slices of bread and listened to Lettice ramble on about her kids.

"Those neighbours of mine just got it in for Tommy Junior because he lit off some firecrackers under their stoop last fall. It was just for a bitta fun at Hallowe'en. Some people can't take a joke, ya know?"

I'd had a couple of firecrackers lit under me this morning, I decided, shuddering.

"Winny," I said, "Percy once told me there were only two families who owned this place before us. Right?"

"That's right." She dug her knife into the mustard.

"There were the Parkses before us, right?"

"Yep. Mary and Bill. They loved this place. Bill died about five years ago. Mary carried on until she had her stroke. Their son, Walter, didn't want it—even with Percy as manager. Not enough money for greedy old Walter."

"So...uh..." I stammered, "what about the *first* family?"

She spread mustard on a piece of bread. "I don't know much about this place back then. I came here from Saskatchewan to teach school. When I was in my thirties. Percy was already working for the Parkses. Let's see...that first family..."

"Shaw!" Lettice said loudly. "That was their name, Winny."

A chill shivered through my body. I stared at Lettice. "S-Shaw?"

She nodded. "I know, cause my gran run the store up at Rosewood. And she knew everyone. That Mr. Shaw was a remmutance man, Jess."

"A what?"

"A remittance man," Winny said. "Younger sons of the

rich English who were given money to settle in Canada. The eldest son usually inherited the family estate. So the others had to fend for themselves. Poor babies. Came with bags of Daddy's money to make new lives. I heard they could be pretty wild. Polo. Horse racing — wasted lives. Didn't have a clue what they were doing. Still, there were some who became good solid ranchers."

Lettice nodded her agreement. "That's right! You know lots, Winny, don'tcha?"

"Your gramma knew the Shaws?" I asked Lettice.

"Well, sort of. We been here as long as anyone, I figure. My gramma ran the store for old Mr. Oster. Everyone would come in and tell her all the news. Those Shaws didn't last long."

"How come, I wonder?"

"There was this really weird mystery about the end of their livin' around here." She screwed up her eyes and thought intently. "I can hear my gramma now." Lettice's voice took on an aged, cracked tone. "'That poor Mr. Shaw,' she'd say. 'Stuck out here to live with that stiff-necked young wife. Made his life a misery.'"

Winny rolled her eyes.

"No one liked Missus Shaw," Lettice went on. "Her dad was a Sir somebody or other in the old country. Out here that didn't mean a darn thing. She hated it over here. She hated ranching. And as for the boy — well..."

I felt my scalp tighten. "The boy? They had a boy?"

"That's what the mystery's about. One minute them Shaws was here and the next minute they was gone. And when people come lookin', they found a fresh grave up on the hill." Lettice lowered her voice. "My gramma said the boy was sickly and no one got to see him much. Mr. Shaw left a note for his neighbour, John Parks, giving him all the animals and the house and everything. And then—poof!— he just vanished."

I gulped hard. "And his wife...went with him?"

Lettice looked mysterious. Or tried to, with her lips turned down and her eyes squinting. She whispered loudly, "Word came to my gramma that the man left alone. Some said he told old Mrs. Parks they both died—the boy *and* his mama. But the wooden cross over the grave never had no name on it. 'Course, it's long gone and the grave's grown over. Can't even tell where it was any more. But my gramma, for one, held that Missus Shaw killed herself after the boy took sick and died."

I must have looked as demented as Lettice, because Winny said loudly, "Jess, don't believe everything Lettice tells you. Good grief! Lettice, just how much of this are you making up?"

Lettice's freckled face turned red. "I'm not makin' nothin' up! My gramma used to tell me stories every night. And the one about the Shaws was the one I liked the most. It were so inneresting. See, no one was ever told what was in Mr. Shaw's note." She turned to me and lowered her voice. "Bill Parks' dad, John, got this place from Mr. Shaw and he give it to Bill and Mary. The note was attached to the land deed. My gramma knew that for sure! And I'm telling Jess just what my gramma told me, Winny! And my gramma weren't no liar!"

"Okay. Okay, calm down for Pete's sake," Winny said, piling sandwiches on big wooden platters.

Lettice continued to mutter angrily, but I tuned her out. If she was right about the story she was defending so fiercely, then two people had died in this house and no one knew when or how. Could it be that both of them were still wandering around this house? If so, what did they want from Mom? Or me?

❧ ❧ ❧

Willow Creek Ranch, Alberta, 1908, May 16
Today, I lay in bed a little later than usual. A feeling of utter freedom seemed to surround the entire ranch, cloaking it in a bright peacefulness which I had never experienced before. I was just dozing off when Father came upstairs and demanded that I be ready to go in the buggy in one half-hour exactly. He sounded almost angry. Where on earth were we going? It took much longer than usual to dress myself, as my fingers had all turned to thumbs. When I made it downstairs, Father was waiting beside the buggy.

We travelled for more than an hour, Father's brown mare, Lally, trotting tirelessly along the dusty wheel track, past the village of Rosewood, through the valley and along the other side. Father never said a word until we approached the wide wooden gate of John Parks' ranch, the Double E.

"I think I can count on your discretion, can't I, old chap? You won't tell her about our little outing?" Father asked.

I shook my head vigorously. "No, Father. Never."

"Good," Father said, nodding. He clicked his tongue and Lally moved forward.

As we drove down the narrow dirt road towards the ranch house, I gazed around with pleasure. The sky stretched from horizon to horizon like a billow of luminous blue silk. Woven into its edges were the fringes

117

of dark trees that ringed the valley. The air here was clear and light with the scent of clover.

As we approached the ranch house, a small group of horses, filled with the spirit of the day, ran first one way and then the other across the field. Suddenly, turning as one, they galloped up to the fence to watch Lally and her passengers trot closer. When our buggy passed by, one small horse, grey as a thundercloud, broke free and trotted along the fence, keeping pace with Lally, who, as all good Morgans do, ignored this brash upstart.

Then something came to me. This little grey horse... it looked like...

"Father..." I began, "that grey horse—"

Father took off his broad-brimmed hat and dropped it over my head. "Well, dear boy," he said. "A good rancher knows his own horse. How do you like him?"

I pushed the hat back from my eyes and gaped at the grey, who wheeled and pranced beside us, whinnying loudly.

"You mean—? Is it, Father? You didn't sell him? Is that why you couldn't account for the money?"

Father laughed. "I've only broken one promise in my life, Ian. And this is going to be the second." For a moment his face clouded over. "And I shall go on breaking this one."

I've only remembered those words now, as I write them down. I have to fight to keep the meaning of his reckless words from overtaking all my happiness. For *She* will return. She will find out. But this morning, what bliss! My very own horse! He danced beside us, his head high, mane streaming out behind. If I am dreaming now, may I never wake up!

CHAPTER 13

I WAS SO DEEP IN MY THOUGHTS ABOUT THE SHAWS AND ghostly houses and flickering lights that I jumped a mile when the back door swung open and three canvas bags were pitched through it. Right behind the gear came my father. His new cowboy hat and clothes looked as if a herd of steers had tromped on them. Boots gummed thick with mud, he stood inside the door — defeated, exhausted.

Winny looked at the clock. "You're home early."

"Early! Rain for two solid days, trails slick with mud, fires that wouldn't stay lit. I have fourteen miserable riders out there who hate my guts and you wonder why I'm early?" Dad threw his hat on the huddled pile of soggy stuff. "Jess, come here and get these damn boots off me. I've had them on since I left. I think they've grown onto the soles of my feet." He looked for all the world as if he was about to collapse into tears.

I bit my bottom lip to keep the giggle under control. The boots were way too big for him. His feet must have been sliding back and forth in them all weekend. No wonder they hurt. Men can be so dumb. He gripped the doorframe and moaned with relief as each socked foot hit the floor.

"Coffee, Mr. Locke?" boomed Winny. "If you can make it as far as the table, you might even get a bite to eat."

Dad glared at her and groped his way to the nearest chair. From the way he was walking, I think his backside hurt more than his feet. The screen door creaked open again and Percy poked his head in. "I seen the others headin' for their cabins. Just talked to Ben. Some trouble?"

Dad was sitting at the table, his face in his hands, letting the steam from the coffee float up to him. He nodded and groaned. I had never seen my father look so physically broken and so...well...funny at the same time. The giggle rose again and I coughed to cover it up.

Percy took his hat off and accepted a cup of coffee from Winny.

When they looked at each other, I could see they were having the same problem I was. Percy reached over and slammed Dad gently on the back.

"Hey, don't let it worry you none there, Glen. Those people know it's part of the deal. As long as you filled their bellies and kept 'em warm at night, they'll pay up happily enough."

Dad moaned. "The tents—especially the cook tent. We had pancakes and water, not pancakes and syrup. I told them I'd give them the weekend for half-price."

Percy's hairpiece shifted back and forth with repressed merriment, but he kept his voice serious. "I warned you about them tents. But you wouldn't fix 'em."

Dad muttered, "I know, I know, I know. I just didn't think it would rain the first time out. I figured I could replace them a few at a time."

"Well, why don't we do it this way," said Percy. "That

120

fella who repairs canvas I told you about — we'll take 'em over to his shop tomorrow and get 'em fixed. You'll still be able to use 'em for a while. That'll give you time to order some of those new nylon types. It'll cost you, but it'll be worth it."

Dad looked up. "You think that'll work? Yeah, that would work, wouldn't it? Thanks, Percy, I'd appreciate that." He looked uncomfortable for a moment, then muttered, "Maybe we could talk about ... about what else went wrong. I've got to figure out how to keep this from happening again."

"You can't stop the rain, Glen, but you can work and ride in comfort if you know what you're doin'."

Dad looked like a little kid. "And you'll help me?"

Percy nodded. "All you have to do is ask."

Just then the phone rang. "Yes, yes we do, ma'am," said Winny. "No, no, that shouldn't be a problem. Let me just check our book here." She covered up the receiver with her hand. "A summer camp over by Bragg Creek wants to know if they can book two day-trips. About ten kids each. Next Thursday and Friday. Okay?"

Dad leaped to his feet. "Day-trips? Of course, of course! Tell them yes."

And just like that, Dad was back to a good imitation of his old self. Striding up and down, making plans, talking about advertising, telling Percy that you had to get right back on the horse when you fell off, wasn't that right? Percy nodded seriously. Winny began cutting the rest of the sandwiches for the guests. I did the same. Lettice sat and stared at Dad until Winny nudged her to get back to work.

"I can shower later," Dad said. "Right now, you and I are having an executive meeting, Percy. Right here! Maybe full stomachs will keep the guests from wanting to drink my blood! I'll talk to them and say goodbye when they're on their second coffee. And give us a big pile of sandwiches, too, Winny, because your good husband's going to need all his strength. I intend to pick his brain clean."

Was I hearing right? For the first time ever, my father seemed to be admitting he didn't know what he was doing. But before I could get too carried away in admiration, a terrible thought hit me. I guess, in the back of my mind, I'd figured that we would move on, that Dad would lose interest and we'd go back to Winnipeg. That's probably why I hadn't unpacked.

But Dad had his teeth in this and wasn't going to give up easily. And staying meant I had to figure out the weird things going on in this house. That old hatbox seemed to be the only way to begin.

Why couldn't Dad just admit that he wasn't cut out to be a middle-aged cowboy, so we could get the heck out of here? Instead, there he was, hunched over a pad of paper, scribbling away as he grilled Percy.

While we were putting pickles in bowls, Winny chuckled. "Your dad never says die, does he?"

"Yeah," I said sadly, thinking about Scotty and Mom and the Shaws. "It looks as if no one around here ever says die."

❦ ❦ ❦

Willow Creek Ranch, Alberta, 1908, May 16
This cool spring night seems endless. Each time I wake up, it is the moon and not the sun that has moved slowly across my window, spreading silvery, ever-changing patterns across the dark floor. So I have lit my candle and here I sit, scribbling away.

Tomorrow — tomorrow I will ride my horse for the

122

very first time. I smile into the darkness, the toes of my good foot curling in ecstasy. *She* will never know — she must *never* know that on this night my lovely dapple-grey beast is wandering like a phantom shadow across the dark meadow below. *My* horse. I imagine he is sleeping under one of the trees, his long neck arched towards the ground, his muzzle deep in the moist grass. He is so beautiful.

In a few days he'll be returned to the Double E ranch and into Mr. Parks' care. I will be able to see him now and again, when Father is free from work. When *She* returns, there will not be a sign left. Only the happiness I feel. I must work hard to keep from giving everything away.

I wriggle further under the warm covers and I can feel my grin almost splitting my face. My very own horse! I have to think of a name for him. Something befitting a cowboy's mount. Star, perhaps, or Lightning? He is the colour of clouds on a stormy day. I suppose I could call him Storm. But remembering the soft velvet nuzzle of his mouth when I fed him sugar lumps this evening, I know he doesn't suit such a violent name. In a way, he is a spirit horse, isn't he? Only made to appear at times like this, when *She* goes away. I have it! I will call him Phantom. It is perfect.

By naming him, he is truly, truly mine. But I feel my heart tighten. As always, whenever one side of me allows for a moment of happiness, the other half, ever watchful of my stern keeper, warns me that the happiness won't — can't — last. She *will* find out.

No. No! I won't give in. Tomorrow I will ride my lovely smoky Phantom. What joy! Father has sworn that *She* will never know. Having Father sharing this secret with me — well, it makes the adventure all the sweeter!

CHAPTER 14

WHEN PERCY WENT TO THE CORRALS TO WORK WITH Ben, Dad remained hunched over his notepad, writing furiously. The phone rang again and Winny answered it. After saying a few words, she looked at me and then at Dad. "Mr. Locke? Glen? It's for you."

Dad waved a hand at her. "Tell whoever it is I'm busy. I'll call them back or you can take the particulars and—"

"It's the doctor. About your wife."

Dad's head swung up sharply. "The doctor? About Jeanie? What doctor? What's wrong?"

Winny said quietly, "Doctor Ambrose wants to talk to you." She held out the receiver.

Dad walked to the phone grumbling, "What's he want? What am I supposed to say to him? Hello? Hello? Yes?"

The doctor must have had a lot to say, because Dad's face grew stiffer and stiffer. With narrowed eyes, he looked from Winny to me and back again. The few words he managed to squeeze in were things like, "Yes. Yes. No, I didn't know," —and— "They didn't tell me. Yes, I see."

My chest tightened. I knew that look settling on his face.

It was his nobody's-going-to-tell-me-how-my-family-should-live face. He was getting really mad. Just when I was sure he'd hang up in a rage, the doctor must have said something that finally got through to him, because he frowned and I saw real alarm in his eyes.

Lettice whispered, "I bet Doc Ambrose is never going to shut up, eh? He does that when he's upset, Jess. Just goes on and on. I bet your dad—"

"Lettice!" snapped Winny. "Take off. I'll see you tomorrow. Bright and early, mind."

"But Winny—" Lettice whined.

"Go on. Out!"

Lettice slid slowly off her stool, listening hard.

Winny grumbled and pointed at the door. Lettice moved a little faster, calling out, "Well, so long everyone." The screen clacked shut, but a second later she was back, her face pressed against the mesh.

Winny sighed. "Lettice!"

"No, no, Winny, I'm going," Lettice croaked. "It's just that Mrs. Locke is coming up the road. Hi there, Mrs. Locke," she called. Then peering in at us again, she whispered loudly, "She's almost here!"

"It's okay, Lettice," I said. "See you tomorrow. Mom's just been for a walk."

Lettice nodded and waved goodbye. We could hear her talking loudly and a few seconds later Mom walked in.

Dad, still on the phone, gaped at the sight of her. There was Jeanie, dressed for the first time in weeks. It wasn't a great outfit, a pair of ancient jeans, a limp sweater covered in lint balls and a pair of scuffed old Rockports. But, she was up, dressed, and coming in the back door.

"Yes. If you insist," Dad said into the phone, "but I think you are overreacting, okay? For Jeanie's sake, I'll see she comes. Yes, I'll bring her, but I think it's a waste of time. You want to know how she's doing?" He got a smug look on his face. "She's just come in from outside. Been for a walk from the look of her. Yes, isn't it. Goodbye." And he hung up.

The smug look vanished. "What went on here yesterday?" he demanded. There was no 'How are you, Jeanie,' or 'Gee it's good to see you up.' That wouldn't be Dad. "And who is this Hodge character the doctor mentioned? Ben's uncle — or grandfather or whatever. If they're going to come here upsetting my family, Ben'll have to go! And where have *you* been?" he demanded of Mom.

Typical. Ask a million questions but don't wait for any answers.

"I went out for a long walk. To think," Mom said, resting one hand on the counter as if she was out of breath.

"Did you eat some breakfast? Or lunch?" His face was a deep red. "Have you been out all this time without anything in your stomach? Look at you. You're as thin as a rake. Your jeans are hanging off you."

Mom pulled on her sweater and looked defiant. "I am about to eat some lunch. Was that Doctor Ambrose? What did he say?"

"Thanks to everybody here, I had no idea about this... episode... yesterday," he snapped. "Needless to say, I felt like a bloody fool."

"But did he tell you about this — his friend — psychologist?" she asked. "He said she might be able to help me. To help Scotty and me."

Dad's eyes bulged. "Help — ?" He ran his hand over his face. "Look. I've just had a terrible weekend. Could this wait until the guests have gone and then we can talk about it? Logically? And *rationally*?"

126

Mom's mouth twisted to one side. "Sure. Why not? First things first, eh, Glen?"

Suddenly, before our eyes, she turned the colour of putty.

"Mom!" I cried out, catching her as she slid to the floor.

"Don't panic," Winny said loudly. "She's just fainted. Hasn't eaten for a couple of days."

Mom moaned and her eyes fluttered open. Dad reached down to pick her up, but I got to my feet and pushed him with all my might. He staggered back against the counter, knocking a jar of pickled onions into the sink with a loud crash.

"Don't you touch her!" I cried.

Winny helped Mom to her feet and led her to the back stairs, talking quietly and soothingly.

"Jeanie?" Dad called out, shaking pickle juice off his hands.

"It's okay, Glen," Mom replied in a soft breathless voice. "I'll be okay. You go back to your guests. Help with the lunch. Winny'll bring me up some soup and tea. I need to rest now."

And with that she was gone.

Dad swung around, his voice ominous. "Jess, damn you, what — !"

"You heard Mom," I snarled. "You'd better grab some sandwiches and start serving your guests. I can hear them in the dining room. They'll be wondering what the shouting's all about. What kind of a reputation will this place get?"

"Hell and damnation!" he said, grabbing a plate and diving for the door. "But I'm not through with you yet, young lady!"

"And *Father Dear*, I'm not through with you, either," I called. With that, I shoved the back door open and ran out.

127

❧ ❧ ❧

Willow Creek Ranch, Alberta, 1908, June 1
She is back. She returned a bare two weeks after she had
driven away with Mr. Gallagher. My work was stacked
neatly on my desk. Father and I have had a bit of a lark
over that. We stayed up for two nights, almost all
through each night, getting it done. While she looked it
over, I watched her. Would she be able to tell I hadn't
done it all myself? Oh, the writing was mine, but even
so...

She looked up at me now and again, eyes narrowed,
but she said nothing until she was done. Then she set
the work aside and said, "It looks as if you can handle a
little more of a challenge. It could be neater, but you've
managed to get more done than I ever imagined. Did
your father help?"

I decided that a half truth was better than a complete
lie. "When I got stuck a bit, he helped," I murmured.

"Very well. Come to supper. Madeline has prepared a
roast. She's behaving oddly. She defies me with her eyes.
Do you know why?" She watched me closely.

I sat very still, my heart pounding. Father had offered
to pay Madeline for her silence about the horse, but she
had pushed his hand and the money away. "The boy has
need of fresh air and sunshine. I will say nothing."

Would she keep her promise? I gulped and shook my
head. "Madeline seems just as always," I said, but my
voice was stiff and unnatural, even to my own ears.

"She hasn't had a man calling on her, has she?" she
demanded.

I didn't know how to answer. Madeline and I had
talked often during the two weeks. Sometimes, she had

allowed me to help her prepare the meal. I liked that very much. She told me that she had been brought up in an orphanage in Calgary and that she was half English and half Sarcee. She had no family. Her mother had died when she was very young, but even so, she remembered her. "I am missing her all my life," she said. I said I was sorry and she nodded, but then she looked at me sadly and I knew that she felt more sorry for me than I ever could for her.

A few days ago, while we were in the kitchen, one of Father's farm hands came in and tried to talk to her. She stared at him as if he was a spider and he soon left. Only when she looks at Father do I see some life in those dark eyes. Or when she looks at me. I think she likes both of us. As we do her.

So when *She* asked me again about Madeline and whether or not a man had called on her, I sat up and said firmly, "No. No one has been here but Father and Madeline and me. The two men Father hired to help with the barn repairs have been gone for more than a week."

She took a pile of papers and tapped them on the desk, making sure they were in order. "You can be as coy as you wish. Butter may not melt in your mouth now, but something went on here when I was away. Your father is acting in a furtive manner. Madeline is almost insolent. And you—you have done more work in two weeks than you've done in six months. I'll find out, Ian. You mark my words. And when I do, we'll see who will pay the price for any deceit that has been performed during my absence."

I listened to her heels tapping sharply down the hall. I

sat staring at my hands for a long time, feeling the tug of that awful darkness that had filled my days before she left. Will everything go wrong again? Will she ruin everything? No! I won't let it happen.

CHAPTER 15

A S I PEERED INTO THE STABLE, THE CONCENTRATED smells of animal, hay and straw wet with urine smacked into my nose.

I heard a low murmur.

"Percy?" I called.

"I'm over here," someone grunted.

I walked down the concrete pad between the rows of stalls, past the rounded glossy rumps of three horses, each in its own stall. The light in the low-roofed space seemed heavy—thick with shadows, full of dust and flecks of straw and washed all over with an amber mistiness.

Percy was hunkered down beside Cocoa, applying something to her leg. He glanced up at me and smiled, his face wrinkling into a million tiny lines in the glancing light. With a groan, he straightened up, patted Cocoa's rump and screwed the top on a big jar.

"Vet was here again. She'll be fine."

"Good." I stood, hands in my pockets, trying to decide how to start.

"Your mom's up and around, I see," he said, adjusting his

tractor cap. "There'll be trouble when your dad calls Doctor Ambrose, I'll bet, eh?"

No beating around the bush with Percy. I grimaced. "The doctor just called him. Dad couldn't decide who to strangle first. Mom fainted."

Percy glared. "Your pa cause that?"

"I don't—yeah, he did. But she hadn't eaten all day. And I think the long walk didn't help. Dad just went on and on at her. He never gives anyone a chance."

Percy chewed on his moustache for a moment, then shook his head. "Your pa. He's got his problems, doesn't he? Himself bein' the biggest one. Your mom okay?"

"Winny's with her."

"How does she seem to you, your mom?"

Putting it into words was hard. "I—I'm not sure. I mean, when she looks at me she's seeing me, you know? And when she talks to me, she uses my name and I know she's talking to *me*." My voice shook a little. "But, sometimes I feel like I'm the mother. If only Dad would—if only... Jeez, he makes me so mad."

"You know, I wouldn't tell this to anyone else, but my Winny went through a tough time quite a few years back. Only, it was because we couldn't have kids. We had a couple of foster kids we was hopin' to adopt. But the social worker just come one day and took 'em—two years they'd been with us—it almost killed Winny. She really loved those kids. She was plenty depressed for a long time, I can tell you."

"How did you help her?"

He shook his head. "I didn't. We both needed help. I loved them kids, too. But it almost split Winny and me apart. Men ain't supposed to grieve the same as women. I just left. Not for good, but I found work that took me away

132

for longer and longer — takin' rich Americans through the hills for weeks on end or drivin' a truck for a fella I knew." He leaned towards me. "Now, I'm pretty ashamed of myself, Jessica. I shoulda stayed with Winny through it all. She didn't seem to want me around, but I shoulda stayed. Lucky for me, time passed and things righted themselves. Like I said, I wouldn't tell just anyone. But your dad reminds me a bit of myself back then."

I was astounded. "Dad?"

"You figure he ain't helpin' your mom. Well, maybe he can't. Maybe he thinks he's gotta be the strong one. Or could be he's just runnin' away, too."

"Dad's always been like this. He does what *he* wants, not what anyone else might want. He doesn't even realize that he forced Scotty —" I wrapped my arms around my chest. "He's ignoring Mom because he doesn't want his life upset by someone being sick. So he pretends it isn't happening. I know my dad. You don't."

I sounded snarly, but I couldn't help it. I'd seen what he'd done to Mom when she'd needed him most.

Percy patted my shoulder. "You think about what I said. No one gives lessons on how to handle the loss of a young one. And you can tuck that stubborn little chin back in — I'm finished my lecture. Besides, when you come in here, you looked like you had somethin' else on your mind."

Still a little miffed, I was going to deny it, but I had to ask or I'd never find out anything. "Oh. Yeah. Well . . . I wanted to ask you — Winny says you may know something about the people who used to live here."

"You mean the Parkses? Mary and Bill Parks?"

"No. The first family. The Shaws."

Percy walked over to a half-full wheelbarrow and pushed it towards a pile of dung. He took the shovel out of the barrow and leaned on it. "The Shaws? Now who told you their name was Shaw?"

"Lettice." I waited, because he was nodding slowly, lost in thought.

"Old John Parks got this place offa Mr. Shaw. His neighbour. My grandpa and my parents knew them both." He smiled. "My grandpa was from the old country. Wales. Got a small piece of land just on the other side of Bear Valley. We called him Old Da."

He leaned back and the smile widened. "Old Da loved a good laugh and a good song. My own dad was the same. My grandma was dead when I was born and Mother ran the place. Big woman. Like Winny. We had good times as kids."

His eyes half closed with reminiscence, and for just a second I saw the lined face as it must have been when he was young. Thin and brown, with maybe a shock of black hair.

"But you don't have a ranch now."

"Wasn't much of a ranch then, either. Too small. And when all the men in your family are off ridin' the hills explorin' or leadin' huntin' expeditions, you don't build it up. When Mother died, Old Da followed soon after. By then we was in the Depression years. Dad sold his stock and went off somewhere—never saw him again. Didn't blame him. He missed the two of them—Mother and Old Da— missed 'em so much, he told me, he had to leave. Went off into the mountains. I was brought up by my aunt and uncle. When I was old enough, I started as an outfitter. By the time I was thirty, I had six men workin' for me and I was doin' fine. I met Winny when I was giving Bill Parks a hand here. Time to settle down, I decided." He winked at me. "Parks needed someone to lead the trips at this place. We got along

134

good, the two of us. When he died, I managed the place for Mary. She was quite a worker, that one." He sighed. "I shoulda quit years ago, but I like workin' and that's the way it is."

I wondered how I could get him back to the Shaws, but as usual Percy was ahead of me. He straightened up and said, "Now about these Shaws. My mother knew young Nigel Shaw's wife. Before I was born, a'course."

"What was her name?" I asked uneasily.

"Augusta. Augusta Shaw. She kept herself to herself, Mother said. Augusta sometimes nursed the women through childbirth—she'd had some trainin' in birthin', it was said. Mother had a sort of fascination with Mrs. Shaw when she was young. Mother's people owned the land right next to this, opposite side to the Parkses. Hard to believe it was all pasture land over the rise. Now half of it's forest. Trees are creeping back in." He smoothed his moustache. "A real lady, I remember her saying about Augusta. 'Course Mother was just a child when the Shaws left. But there was dark talk. About Mrs. Shaw. And about her boy."

I felt my pulse quicken. She had a name now. Augusta Shaw. "What was his name? The boy's?"

Percy leaned over and shovelled the dung into the wheelbarrow.

"Now, what *was* that boy's name," he said slowly. "I know—Ian. I remember because my mother's youngest brother was brought into this world by Augusta Shaw and he was named after Mrs. Shaw's little boy. It wasn't long after that, I guess, that her and her son died."

"So, they *both* died," I breathed.

Surprise made his eyebrows go up under his cap peak. "What do you know about all this?"

"Lettice said her grandma knew them."

Percy grunted. "And her granny was just as screwy as our Lettice. Don't believe everythin' she says. And for that matter, don't take everythin' I say as gospel either, because I only heard it from my ma when I was no older than you."

"How did the boy...how did Ian die? They said he was sickly."

Percy shook his head sadly. "That's where all the talk comes from. No one knows. One week the family was here, the next week they were gone. It was midsummer and the cattle were just left grazin'. John Parks came over and found a letter on the table. Right here at this house. John kept the part of the letter that left him the ranch and the cattle, and burned the rest. But later, when someone from town was ridin' up along one of the hills back there, they found a grave. That's when folks put two and two together."

"And they could both be in that grave?" I asked, not sure I wanted an answer.

"No one knows for certain. But the story about *him* dying—the boy—well, it kept buildin'. A young woman who worked for them told someone that the boy died first, the mother later. And I guess like most sad stories, this one got embroidered some. But my mother maintained that John Parks' wife, Edwina, told a few people that Augusta had killed the boy. He musta only been about twelve or so."

"But why did she kill him!"

Percy looked at me kind of funny and I realized how loud I must have shouted. He pointed to the wheelbarrow. I wrapped my hands around its handles and followed him outside.

"You got a reason for all this interest in the boy? In the whole Shaw family?"

"I like history," I said hastily. "And Lettice made it sound like a real mystery. She said the mother sort of disappeared.

136

And then she talked about the boy and his dying and I felt sad. Scotty...the boy—two kids the same age. I guess I was hoping this...Ian, hadn't died. You know? I was hoping it wasn't true."

After we'd dumped the manure, Percy pulled out a small tin box and a penknife. He cut himself a wad of chewing tobacco and carefully pushed it into his cheek. "You really want to know about this boy. Ian Shaw."

I nodded. "I have to know."

He pulled on the peak of his cap. "Like I said, Jessica, I can tell you only what Mother heard from her mother, my Gramma Budgen. Augusta Shaw helped Gramma Budgen durin' the birth of four of her kids, you see."

"That's good enough for me."

"Well, accordin' to Mother and Gramma Budgen, this Augusta was from a fancy family in England. With one of them titles. And her husband, Nigel, was educated at one of them private schools. Maybe after they were married, he got the itch to become a cattle baron. Who knows? As for Augusta, well, she hated it out here."

"Hated it?"

"Yep. And I mean just that. Had her nose in the air when it came to most everything around here. But she was the best midwife in the area. Anyways, Augusta Shaw told my gramma that she intended her son to go to one of those high-class schools in England, like his father. No way was this boy goin' to our one-room schoolhouse, she said, so she took over his schooling herself."

"Augusta taught Ian at home?"

Percy nodded. "Yep. And word was, she kept the boy on a tight rein. Hours and hours of book work every day. No learnin' about the cattle and no ridin'. But most people understood that."

I frowned. "Why?"

"The boy was a cripple. Can't call them that nowadays, Winny says. Anyhow, one leg or maybe both legs was shrivelled up from what I heard. According to Edwina Parks, Bill's old mother, the boy was kept up in his room all the time—that room your mom's in, I believe."

My brain felt as if little electric sparks were flashing all through it.

"He used to look out that window at the men workin' below, my mother said, like a little prince in a castle tower. The fellas talked about the sad face peerin' out at 'em."

My breath was coming in painful little gasps. "How— how did she—how did she—he..."

"How'd the boy die? What happened to his mama? As I said, no one knows. After Nigel Shaw left, no one heard from him again." Percy looked closely at me. "Are you okay there, Jessica? You look white as a ghost."

I tried to laugh and failed. "Do I? I guess I'm hungry. I— I think I'll go get a sandwich or something. The guests are leaving. See? That's the third car in a row. Well, thanks, Percy. I'll get going. If I don't get something to eat, I'll faint...like Mom. Not really... just kidding..."

Turning with a fluttery wave, I ran towards the house. Unfortunately, Dad was standing on the back stoop, waving eagerly at one of the cars as it rumbled past him. I veered sharply behind the stable and leaned on the back wall, eyes closed, mind seething.

Now I was sure. I knew my mother's ghost.

❦ ❦ ❦

Willow Creek Ranch, Alberta, 1908, June 9
The strain is almost more than I can bear. The only thing that keeps me going is remembering those few days that

138

I rode Phantom. *She* watches me all the time now. Unknown to her, I am keeping just as close a watch on myself. My work is done on time. I eat what is put before me. I allow her into my room without argument. The key, however, remains hidden behind the wall by the window sash. I have stopped looking out the window and concentrate only on the work at hand. I stay away from Madeline and Father as much as possible. Worry creases Father's face, but I try to signal with a smile that all is well. It isn't, of course. I worry all the time. I feel the strain all the time.

Sometimes, when I am alone, I allow myself the indulgence of memory. But never during the day. For if I thought about Phantom and Father and the rides around the corral and the lessons on trotting—if I thought about the special saddle, brown and shiny as dark caramel toffee, with its long leather casing to hold my bad leg firmly against Phantom's heaving side—if I thought about all of those things, I know it would show on my face.

Even so, *She* watches—coming into my room more often, even at night. Ever alert, ever vigilant. Once she almost caught me writing in this journal. I was able to slide it under my bed but had a devil of a time retrieving it. She scolds Madeline continuously. She berates Father about the running of the ranch, the accounts, the lack of money. It is as if she is determined to punish us even though she has yet to find out what we have done wrong. Does she want us to hate her? Is that it? Will I never learn what I have done to make her this way?

Will I ever get away from her?

CHAPTER 16

"J EEZ, WHAT A MESS!"

"What's a mess?"

I jumped. Had I spoken out loud? I had been leaning against the fence, chin on my folded arms, lost in miserable thought. Now, somehow, there was Ben on the other side, Prue standing very close to his legs. I smiled down at her.

"Speaking about messes," said Ben, "have you seen your dad?"

I flushed. "I wasn't worrying about my father. I was thinking—oh, never mind."

Ben put his forearms on the railing, a length of rope between gloved hands. His hat was tipped low, the brim almost touching his nose. "I think I saw your mom a little while ago. Over behind the tack shed. She was heading for the house. She okay?"

I nodded. "Yeah, I guess. She—uh—she hasn't been feeling very well since we got here. I guess she overdid the walking today."

An awkward silence drifted down between us. Finally,

Ben pushed away from the rail. For some reason—I didn't know why—I wanted him to talk again, so I said quickly, "So, how did it really go with my dad? You'd think it was the end of the world as he knew it."

Ben's head moved sharply and from under the brim of his hat, his dark eyes looked intently at me. I think I stopped breathing. Then, he smiled—just a quick little quirk at the corner of his mouth. The fence seemed to dissolve under my hands. I looked away quickly, my heart pounding in my throat. Did he have any idea that he could do that to a person? Why me?

Clearing his throat, he said, "He gets upset real easy, doesn't he, your dad? But it wasn't that awful. Just old Mr. Covy gave him a rough time. The others were pretty good about it."

The thought of Dad steadied me. "It sounded *horrible*— rain in the pancakes, dripping tents," I said in disgust.

This time he let out a short bark of laughter but he covered it up fast. "Rain and leaky tents'll do it every time." A loud chorus of whinnying came from the far end of the corral as the horses pushed against the closed gate. "I— uh—I gotta go let them out," he said, turning to go.

"Your grandfather was here yesterday. With your uncle," I called after him, then cringed. Why did I say that?

His shoulders tensed. "So?"

"They—they—that is, your grandfather and Percy, well it was—"

He swung around. "What did Grandpa do?"

"Percy kind of threw him out. You don't have to go home. You can stay here. Winny said so." I swallowed hard. What was I getting myself into?

He scowled and snapped the rope between clenched fists. Percy was waiting for the right time to talk to him and I'd blown it. But did I stop there? No.

"Or you—you can stay with Percy and Winny," I added quickly, feeling heat rise into my cheeks. "They told your—him—that you could stay where you wanted now. But—look, I'm sorry, I—" I was such an idiot!

"Thanks for taking care of Prue," he said stiffly. He whistled to her and they stalked off.

They didn't get far, because Dad called out from the house, "Ben! Hold on there. And I want to talk to you as well, Jess!"

My heart sank. *Now* what?

Dad, flushed with excitement, loped towards us. "Listen, you two, I'm going to need help around here this week. Percy and I sorted out what needs to be done before the next overnight trip. And we just got another call—from a large family in the States. Coming in two weeks. For a whole week! So Ben, I want you to bunk here, in the house. I'll need both of you to take those summer-camp kids out with me at the end of the week. Thursday and Friday."

He was doing it to me again.

"Listen, Dad, I—" I said loudly, but he went on. I stopped listening. I remembered how high it was on the back of a horse, how the brute would take you wherever *it* wanted to go, scraping your legs against bushes and fences, trotting when you wanted to stop and stopping dead when you wanted to walk. And I remembered the horrible sense of losing control, the dash for home, the ground coming up at me, the pain. I wanted to scream at my father, but I couldn't get enough air.

"Jess isn't used to riding. And I'm not having a girl along who can't pull her own weight. Not when I have to handle a buncha kids." Ben spoke gruffly, almost insolently. Anger released the tightness in my throat, and I sucked in a deep

142

breath. Who the heck did he think he was?

"What?" asked Dad. "Oh. Yeees...well, maybe you're right, Ben. We don't want to louse up any more trips. Maybe we'll have to hire another kid. Do you know someone? Think about it. Still, I want you to take Jess out riding. Every day. Get her used to it. Start tonight. Jess, don't be disappointed if you don't make it out this week. We'll turn you into a cowboy before the summer's over." And with that, he was gone.

I sagged against the fence.

"You don't have to ride tonight," Ben said. "I could see you were...you know...scared."

"I'm not scared!" I snapped. "And I'd pull my weight. I can ride. I just need a bit of practice. And a decent horse!"

"So, you *want* to go tonight? Or do you have to wash your hair or somethin'?" he said, grinning.

"As you've already arranged my life with my father, I suppose we'll have to go," I said haughtily.

Ben shook his head. "Okay by me. Last time I bail you out with your dad, though."

I bristled. "I don't know what you're talking about. I just don't want to go out on long treks when I...when I could be..."

"Scrubbing toilets?" Ben sneered. "Come on, Prue. Let's get some work done."

I was definitely having trouble with my feelings. The sight of his blue-jeaned legs and broad back made my heart tip in my chest. I couldn't even work up one rude remark to shout after him. In fact, I was having trouble keeping the smile under my teeth from bursting all over my face.

The smile didn't last long. The house loomed ahead of me, belonging to another time and place as well as the here and now. Sunlight flashed off an upstairs window. Mom was in that room. Ian's room. With Ian. Every day we walked the floorboards that Nigel Shaw had probably laid with his own hands almost a hundred years ago. Was he still walking on them?

History books claim to tell you the way things were in the past — but they're just crisp white paper and black ink. Past times are dusty flowers and mouldering hatboxes and crackling negatives of old photos. And dead people who won't stay dead.

❦ ❦ ❦

Willow Creek Ranch, Alberta, 1908, July 11
A month has gone by. Until today I was too afraid to write anything more in this journal. *She* has not left me alone for long enough to risk it. I know something is going wrong. Inside me. I do my work. I sleep very little. The thought of food makes me ill. I miss Phantom.

Today she announced she has to go away again. Right now she is busy packing. At first, I felt a spark of energy and hope. But then she told me that I will be going with her. We leave tomorrow for a ranch on the other side of Whisky Valley.

Phantom will forget me. I will never ride again.

CHAPTER 17

DAD WALKED QUICKLY OUT OF THE STABLE CALLING instructions over his shoulder to Percy. I waited by the side of the tack shed before following him into the house. When I walked through the kitchen door, Mom was sitting at the table cutting tomatoes.

"*What* are you doing?" Dad asked, radiating disapproval.

"I'm preparing a salad," Mom said, slowly and evenly. Her hair was tied into a tight braid, her face colourless, the shadows under her eyes pale-blue bruises.

"I can *see* that, Jeanie. I've got eyes in my head. But you should be lying down, love. Winny doesn't need your help."

Winny stirred something on the stove and snorted. Mom concentrated on her tomato.

Dad let out an exasperated sigh. "Honestly, Winny, she fainted less than an hour ago."

I could feel the teeth-gritting control that kept Winny from clouting him with her wooden spoon.

"I *insisted* on coming down, Glen," Mom said, in a slow, firm voice. "Winny and I both think I can begin doing a

little bit around the house. I—I have to. Otherwise—"
Her voice shook.

Dad threw up his arms. "I can see I'll have nothing to say about this, so I may as well shut up."

Why didn't he listen, instead of being such a jerk?

"So, are we all eating together?" he asked, picking at the salad.

Mom, keeping her head down, answered, "Why not?" Her hands trembled a little.

Dad looked sharply at Winny. "No reason. Just a simple question."

Winny began mashing potatoes hard and quick. "If you would prefer, Percy, Ben, and I can eat out here in the kitchen from now on, like obedient servants."

"Don't be ridiculous," snapped Dad. "I didn't see any places set here, that's all. I'm going to get a drink. Do you want one, Jeanie? No? Well, tell Percy to join me when he gets here."

"We'll be eating in exactly five minutes," said Winny. "So don't go into one of your planning sessions. I don't want my steak pie and mashed potatoes waiting at an empty table."

Dad grumbled something I couldn't hear and wandered off, stopping to pour himself a drink on the way to the dining room. I suddenly realized why Winny got away with saying just about anything. Dad wouldn't be able to go on if she left—taking Percy with her—and he knew it. Winny winked at me. She knew it, too.

A second later, Percy and Ben walked in. Ben's face was red. Percy looked pretty grim. I was sure they'd been talking about Ben's grandfather's visit. Things did not look good all around.

I whispered to Mom, "Are you really feeling up to this?"

146

She gripped my arm. "Did you tell your father about Scotty?"

"No. No. I promise, I didn't. But—"

"But what?"

"I have something to tell you. Something sort of weird. But it'll have to be later."

"Yes—yes, later," she said, arranging and rearranging the tomatoes on top of the salad. "I—I...think maybe I have to face...that it's all in my...you know...my mind." I saw a strange fevered look in her eyes.

"I'm not sure, Mom. I think something *is* happening in this house. Something that—"

"What do you mean? What is it?" Her voice was high and anxious.

"That's enough yakking, Jess," a voice boomed.

Winny, her face dark as thunder, picked up the salad bowl, shoved it into my hands and pointed towards the dining room. She was right. I shouldn't have upset Mom. My certainty that the Shaws were haunting the house was based on very shaky evidence. If *I* wasn't sure what was real, how could Mom tell? Which of us was hallucinating? Both of us? My mind collapsed. Jess the Robot carried loaded serving dishes into the dining room.

Five minutes later, we all sat down at the big family table in the main dining room. I wished I had one of the smaller tables all to myself.

With pursed lips, Winny scooped big sections of steak and kidney pie onto each plate and then passed around bowls of peas, baby carrots and potatoes. Percy carefully loaded his plate before passing each bowl to my mother with a gentlemanly nod. Mom, pale and wide-eyed, was looking at her food as if a spider might be hiding under the mashed potatoes. Why, why hadn't she stayed upstairs?

147

Dad drained the glass of whisky and sniffed his steaming plate. "This smells absolutely fabulous, Winny." Forking up a chunk of meat, he chewed thoughtfully and moaned with pleasure. "I haven't had steak and kidney pie for years. Not since Jeanie and I went to England. Remember how great the food was in that little hotel in Somerset, Jeanie?"

For once he'd said the right thing. Mom nodded and looked with new interest at her food. Percy nudged Ben and Ben, mouth full, said, "Yeah, Winny...great."

Of course it was too good to last. Dad leaned his elbows on the table and pointed his fork at Percy. "By the way, I can't say I was too impressed with that doctor."

Winny, Percy and I stared. Mom looked up from poking at her potatoes. "You mean Doctor Ambrose?"

Dad shook his head, looking surprised. "Ambrose? No. Some kid named Brooks. New vet."

Mom's eyes dulled. "Oh. I thought...never mind."

"Brooks says Cocoa won't be fit for at least two weeks," Dad continued. "Do you think Poppy, that Appaloosa, will be able to take over? I rode her this weekend and she seemed to fidget a lot when the others were behind us. Vets! They spin these things out just to make more money off us." Then he added, his mouth full, "Like therapists and shrinks."

Percy, with a startled look at Mom, began talking about the horses. Had I heard right? Was Dad really more concerned about Cocoa than about Mom? What was this dig at shrinks? Even Dad couldn't be this dense. What was left of my appetite disappeared. Another bite would have choked me.

Ben wasn't having that problem. One arm wrapped around the edge of his plate, he scooped his food in as if he hadn't eaten in weeks. If his head got any lower, his nose would be in his potatoes. His dark hair was spiked and slightly wet. Even his nails had been scrubbed clean. He wore a fresh blue denim shirt. I noticed a spicy aftershave smell when he reached for more bread. Just then, he looked at me and our eyes locked. With horror, I realized no one was talking.

"You kids going out for that ride tonight?" Dad asked, finally.

I felt my heart bump once into my chest wall. "I—I guess so," I muttered, looking down at my plate in confusion.

"Good! That's what I like to hear. You take her for a long hard workout, Ben, and maybe we can use her on the trail soon."

"What do you mean, a long hard workout?" Mom demanded, her knife and fork clattering against the plate. "You aren't going to force her to ride! She isn't ready."

Dad snorted. "For heaven's sake, Jeanie, Jess can't live on a guest ranch and not ride a horse. I can't be laying money out for other people's kids to come here and do what she's perfectly capable of doing. After all, it's a family enterprise. That's what we agreed to."

"Listen, Mom, I—" I started.

"No, Glen," she said, her voice taut. "It is not what *we* agreed to. *I* did not agree to anything and neither did Jess. *You* bought this ranch, Glen. *You* decided it would be our new home. Now *you* can run it."

Dad's smirk staggered off his face. "Hey, take it easy, love. Jess has been doing the odd chore around here already. So, she had a bit of a fall—it wasn't the end of the world." Every word precise—as if he was talking to an idiot. Then his voice softened. "Didn't this Doctor Ambrose give you some kind of pills for when you get excited?

149

Maybe you should take one, eh, Jeanie? Eh, love?"

Mom gripped the edge of the table. "I don't need any damn pill. I am trying to make you see—"

Dad spoke right over her. "I don't know if I like the sound of this Ambrose guy, love. He *says* you need to see this shrink friend of his. But I wonder; I really do. That just might make things worse. Besides, it takes these shrinks years of peering inside your head. There's nothing wrong with you that rest and fresh air won't make better, eh? No one in our family's needed a shrink yet. And I don't think we need one now."

Mom laughed. But not as if what Dad had said was funny. From the murky dullness of her eyes, I saw the glint of something hard and cold.

"You *never* see, do you?" She leaned over her plate. "The reason Jess can't go on those trips with you is because she's working her backside off helping Winny. She's been doing my job *and* her job. She's been covering up for *me*. Because I've been useless. I've been upstairs. Doing nothing!" Her voice broke, the words thick with emotion. "I can't do this on my own. I can't sit up there day after day waiting for... I can't. I don't know—" She slammed both her hands on the table, tears rolling down her cheeks.

Dad said hastily, "It's okay, Jeanie. I'm sorry I said anything. Soon you'll be feeling better, eh, love? Soon—"

She stood up, and her chair rocked back before it settled four-square on its legs with a loud thunk. "Will I? How on earth do *you* know? I don't know. I don't know if I will *ever* get through a day without this... this blackness all around." Her voice caught in her throat. "You... you haven't really talked to me in weeks." She mimicked him. "*You're looking fine, love. Everything okay, love?* But you don't wait for an answer. Sometimes I hear you come up the front stairs, and you don't even put your head around my door. You skulk by, hoping I won't know you're there."

Percy and Winny were exchanging eye signals across the table. Ben looked as if he wished the floor would open up and swallow him.

Dad brushed one hand through the air in front of his face. "But you didn't want—"

In a deadly quiet voice, Mom said, "Don't say another word. Not—one—word—more."

She was staring at something over Ben's shoulder. Then, she caught her breath suddenly, as if she'd been slapped. Wrapping her arms around herself, she began to shake her head back and forth. Dad shifted his chair away from the table.

"I'm okay," she said through shuddering teeth. "He—it comes and goes."

"You go on now, Missy," said Winny, in a firm voice. "I'll bring you up a big cup of hot tea."

Dad said, "Jeanie, can I—"

"No, you can't. Stay where you are."

When she passed by my chair, Mom put a hand on my shoulder. I could feel not just ordinary shivering, but a sort of vibration, deep, deep inside.

"Jeanie!" Dad called. "Look, love, I—"

"Leave me alone, Glen. Just leave me alone."

We watched her walk out of the room. Percy noisily gathered up dishes.

Ben cleared his throat. "I'll go saddle the horses. You come when you want, Jess."

"Winny and me are goin' into Stough Creek to play cards with Frank and Bella Singer. We're leavin' in half an hour," Percy said to Dad stiffly. "Then we'll probably go home for the night just to check on things." To me, he said, "If you need us, call. We can be here in less than ten minutes. Ben knows the Singers' number. And you've got Doctor Ambrose's by the phone there." He looked pointedly at Dad before leaving the room with a rattling load of dishes.

"What brought all that on?" Dad said, finally.

That did it.

"If you kept your big mouth shut and your big ears open, then maybe you'd know." I was shocked that my voice was so calm. "Tell me, Dad, were you *ever* going to notice how sick she's been? Were you *ever* going to listen to us? Are you really going to keep her from getting help, too? Hoping it would all go away — Mom — the doctor — making sure no one interferes with the running of this stupid, stupid ranch? Tell me, Dad, don't you want her to get better?"

He looked as if I'd beaned him with a hard ball. "Now — now you listen here, young lady! Don't you tell me how to behave with my own wife. She — she *asked* me to give her some space. I've — "

"Giving her space doesn't mean leaving her alone day and night!"

"She seems to be getting better. Why, look at her today. She — "

"Mom's been in la-la land for weeks and weeks and you've totally ignored it. This whole mess is your fault! First you make Scotty — "

I stopped, but it was too late.

"Go on," he said, his eyes locked on me.

"Never mind, I — "

"No. Go on, Jess. You may as well say it. You and your mother believe it." His face was grey.

"Look, Dad, no one blames you for... I — I just want you to think about what Mom is going through, okay?"

"I know what your mother's going through! It's what *I'm*

going through. I'm coping with every rotten empty day in the only way I know. I—"

Suddenly, it was as if both of us were struck dumb. I was sure that his next words, or mine, would change everything, that we would actually talk about Scotty and about Mom for the first time. But Winny's voice cut through the deafening silence, and the moment was gone.

"The vet's here. He wants to try a new ointment on Cocoa. He's anxious to talk to you."

I waited for Dad to tell Winny that the vet could wait. Instead he said, "I'll be right there."

He looked over my head and said in a voice that seemed to be squeezed from his throat, "Despite what you think, I've always done what I thought was right—for all of us." His lips moved, stiff and unnatural, as if frozen. "Your mother and I will work things out on our own. I don't need a sixteen-year-old girl telling me how to behave." With that, he strode out of the room.

ಶಿ ಶಿ ಶಿ

Willow Creek Ranch, Alberta, 1908, July 12
A curious thing has happened. This morning, when we were supposed to leave, I couldn't get out of bed. It wasn't deliberate defiance. I simply couldn't get out of bed. Despite dire warnings from *Her*, I couldn't obey. My limbs felt as if the bones had melted. My head was blurry, and a languid, continuous sigh washed through me. It was like nothing I've ever felt before, yet I didn't fear it.

I was alone in the room, facing the wall, with my eyes shut, when I heard a rustling sound. Someone was in the room with me. Had *She* come back? I hadn't heard her

153

approach. The rustle began again and then silence. I rolled over onto my back and forced my eyes open. It wasn't *Her*. And it wasn't Madeline. Instead, the dark eyes of the ghostly stranger looked at me from a pale, misty face. She smiled, but the smile did not reach her eyes.

I tried to smile back but couldn't. She wore an odd robe and her hair stood out from her face like a dark cloud, its edges blurred in the strange light that surrounded her. She leaned over and lay one small white hand against my cheek. I felt a strange peace flow through me. Then, she faded as quickly as she had come.

Almost immediately, *She* walked into the room, Father following right behind. I watched passively while they argued over me.

"He can't go. He's not well," Father said.

"He's putting on a very good act," she answered. "He is going to get out of that bed and come with me. Mr. Eagleton is downstairs and I am not keeping him waiting. Ian! Get up at once."

I stared at the ceiling, pretending I didn't hear. The figure that visited me had given me only momentary courage, not enough to fight *Her*. If she hauled me out of bed and dressed me, I could not fight, but I didn't care, either.

Vaguely, I realized Father was fighting for me.

"And I am telling you the boy is overworked and ill. You've had him at that desk for weeks. He is exhausted. Do you want to kill him?"

Her hand landed with a resounding smack on Father's face. "Don't you *ever* say such a thing to me. I have wanted only the best for him. I don't want him ending up a failure — like you. Where is the grand house you

154

promised me? Where are the mighty herds of cattle and the rows of servants? He is a *cripple*! What will his future be here? He *has* to be prepared for a life that he is suited for."

So that's why she hates me, I thought listlessly. It is because I am a cripple.

"Augusta, for heaven's sake!" Father protested.

"If I don't prepare him, who will?" she cried. "If I don't protect him from injury, who will? You—you would have him ride a horse, of all things! You would risk having him hurt. And you accuse me of trying to kill him? This is the last straw, Nigel. I shall go home. And I will take him with me. You can live here by yourself, riding and dreaming and making nothing of your life." She was white with rage. "Keep him for the few weeks I'll be gone. Because when I return, I will be packing. And he is coming with me!"

She swept out of the room.

CHAPTER 18

"**I**T'S ME. JESS."

I waited, looking straight at the door. I thought of the hatbox one room away, its contents lying scattered on the floor, and was relieved when Mom's door slowly opened. She was back in her housecoat and woollen socks, her hair loose. The room was hot and thick with cigarette smoke. I shut the door.

"Okay if I open the window?" I asked, walking quickly across the room.

"I embarrassed everyone, didn't I?" Mom said listlessly.

I looked out into the yard. "It's okay. I don't blame you. Dad's such a—" I shrugged and slid the window up.

She sat down in her rocker and lit a cigarette. A warm gust from the open window swirled the smoke around me, burning my eyes.

"I shouldn't have done it in front of the others. But— he—it's something I had to say. I should have waited. It wasn't fair."

I shrugged again. "He's not fair, either. All he ever thinks about is himself."

She opened her mouth to say something and then looked away, taking a deep drag on her cigarette. I sat on the edge of the bed, my hands clasped between my knees. I couldn't think how to begin.

Mom slowly rocked. "You had something to tell me?"

I examined the toes of my new riding boots. The leather was deeply scratched and most of the polish was off.

"Jess?"

I chewed on my bottom lip. "It's sort of complicated."

My throat was getting dry from the acrid smoke, my armpits and back were sweating, and I could feel a headache starting.

"Could you put that thing out?" I asked, my voice sharp. "It's like the inside of a cookstove in here."

With a half smile, she ground it into the ashtray. "Well?"

I had planned a little speech, but now it seemed too formal, almost silly. I groped for a way to start. "You said you thought that all of this — this business with Scotty might just be in your head," I said haltingly.

She nodded, her eyes wary. I had to be very careful. I had no proof. Was I seeing Augusta Shaw? Was Mom seeing the boy who had lived and worked in this room? Would I make things worse, talking about Ian Shaw?

"I just thought..." I hesitated, then pushed on. "Well, maybe you *are* seeing *someone* — a boy. He — that is — a boy named Ian Shaw once lived here and — "

"Are you saying I might be seeing...someone *else's* son? A ghost from the past? Are you *serious*?" She was blinking at me in disbelief, as if I'd just told her that Winny was a werewolf.

I stiffened. "It was a long time ago, but Percy says that quite a few old-timers figure Ian died — his mother was — "

Mom stood up. "Have *you* seen him? This — this Ian Shaw?"

I shook my head. "Well, no, but—"

She padded around the room in her socks. Then she sighed deeply and said, "Look, Jess. You're trying to help... I know that... offering me an explanation for seeing Scotty. You needn't worry. I'll sort it out. I'll get the help I need."

"But you said you didn't exactly *see* Scotty. You said you saw what looked like a boy—maybe it..." My voice trailed off.

Mom continued to pace. "No. No, I can't accept what you're saying. I'll only get more bogged down in this— fantasy. I have to fight it. If I'm hallucinating, I have to accept it as a tired mind. The doctor will help. I have to start getting through this mire of—of hopelessness— confusion I'm in."

"Mom, couldn't it be—" I wanted to tell her about Augusta, but she cut me off.

"I know you're only trying to help, honey. Any explanation for the..." Her smile was half finished, hanging in the air like a cold chill. "...for the crazy things I said to you, right? And I thank you, Jess. But I have to fight this. Last night, after we talked, I realized I have to start *fighting*."

I stared at the floor. It was pointless to tell her anything more about Ian. Or Augusta.

"And on that long walk, I decided it was now or never," she continued, her voice thin and low. "But, oh Jess, it's so hard—I'm not sure I'm strong enough to do it alone."

"What about Dad?"

She sat beside me and said softly, "I think, well—I think your dad and I may have... gone too far away from each other."

"But you won't get... divorced, will you? I mean, you'd

158

need a job and we'd have to move again, and—" My voice was high and frightened.

She put an arm around my shoulders. "I'm not ready to make decisions as big as that, Jess. Not yet. I have enough trouble deciding to get up in the mornings, don't I?" She squeezed my shoulder. "It's okay, Jess. Things will work out."

"But what will happen to me?" I blurted.

"We'll always take care of you, honey. We'd never leave you alone."

Before I could stop myself, I cried, "But you already have, haven't you? You already have!"

Her head snapped up. Before she could say anything, I dragged open the door and ran down the hall. She didn't follow.

❧ ❧ ❧

Willow Creek Ranch, Alberta, 1908, July 16
Four mornings after she left, I sat in the parlour by the fire, trying to concentrate on reading a book. I had promised Father that I would get up and dressed each day. It had been a struggle the first few mornings. I was still slightly wobbly, but Madeline had coaxed me to eat — rich broth, eggs and such — and I had finally begun to feel better.

The quiet in the room was suddenly broken by two sounds: the snap of a twig as it exploded in the fire and a distant whinnying. I sat up and listened, then struggled to my feet. Outside, the snigger of one horse was answered by another's shuddering neigh. One of them was Phantom! I knew that sound as well as I knew Father's voice.

159

In my eagerness to get to the windows, one of my wooden canes slipped and clattered to the floor. When I put my hand out, some force in front of me broke my fall. I was able to regain my balance and slowly retrieve my stick. Who—what had caught me? Had the dark-eyed creature from my room come downstairs? I couldn't see anyone but felt a presence very close. I was sure I heard breathing.

"It's Phantom," I said out loud. "Come with me and see!"

I moved towards the window through heavy air. The feeling of someone beside me was still very strong. When I looked out the window, Father was standing under the huge poplar holding Phantom and Lally, his brown Morgan. Both were saddled.

Father beckoned for me to come outside. He nodded and smiled happily. He had made the decision for us. I felt strength come into my body from the force around me. I waved back at Father and called out to Madeline to get my boots. I was going riding!

As soon as I called out, I felt the force around me withdraw. With careful haste, I moved towards the door.

CHAPTER 19

I RAN DOWNSTAIRS TO FIND WINNY AND PERCY FINISHING the dishes.

Winny said, "We're running late. Jess, would you get the last few things off the table and put them away?"

I nodded and walked out of the kitchen, my feet dragging. Putting the salt and pepper on the sideboard, I tossed the napkins into the fake wood box we used for dirty linen.

When I reached for the woven tablecloth, all the colours in the room darkened. The sun was still shining outside, but not on the tables and floor, even though a few moments before the room had been streaked with yellow light.

Behind me, the clattering in the kitchen was muffled and distant. I lifted the tablecloth, but it was like pulling it through thick water. What was happening? Suddenly a heavy weight pressed against me, almost knocking me over. When I regained my balance the weight lifted but I felt myself being slowly pushed towards the windows.

Outside, Ben was leading two horses into the yard. Wait. It wasn't Ben. Whoever it was, he was shorter and dressed in dark pants, a plain shirt and a wide-brimmed hat. Percy? Couldn't be Percy. He was in the kitchen.

The man moved around the horses, pulling on cinch straps and adjusting the stirrups on a heavily muscled brown horse and a dappled grey. They weren't our horses.

The man nodded with satisfaction and tipped the hat back. I strained to make out his features but he and the horses were cloaked in the same murky light that was in the room, as if they were standing in the shade of a non-existent tree.

After patting the grey on the neck, he turned, strangely graceful, like film in slow motion. He gazed directly at the window where I stood. Slowly, slowly, he raised one arm and, looking right at me, he beckoned. His hand scooped the air as if to say, come out, the horses are ready, come ride with me. He was smiling. The light around him suddenly flickered the way sunlight scatters through leaves, and he and the horses seemed to dissolve and reappear in seconds.

Now I knew for certain. There were such things as ghosts — I was looking straight at one. I tried to step back, but the force around my shoulders pressed me towards the window. A confusing mixture of happiness and expectation, anxiety and bewilderment washed through me. I had to fight the urge to go outside.

"Jess? Hey! Jess!"

Every cell in my body froze. The man knew my name.

"You got cotton in your ears?"

I recognized that voice. It wasn't coming from outside. I turned slowly, my eyes searching the room. Ben leaned against the doorframe to the veranda, arms folded, one booted foot crossed over the other.

"Earth to Jess. Come in, Jess."

It was as if his words were being pushed through an invisible wall around me. Then, without warning, the wall dissolved and his voice came through loud and clear.

"So? Are you coming or what?"

I grabbed the window sash and gawked outside. The man and the horses were gone. Tied to the railings were Bower and a small black horse with one white stocking.

Ben's boots thudded across the floor. A hand gripped my shoulder. The warmth spread through my T-shirt. I was so happy to have real flesh and blood touch me, I couldn't speak.

"You okay?"

Swallowing over and over again, I nodded vigorously.

"Do you want to skip the ride?"

I shook my head back and forth.

He cleared his throat. "You — uh — wanna come ... like now?"

I nodded again, my eyes riveted on Bower and the black horse. Ben turned me slowly around. I was surprised to see his dark eyes, gentle and concerned, searching my face.

How could I tell him what I'd seen out that window, or what had happened between Dad and me, or the awful visit with Mom? I fought back humiliating tears.

"You had a fight with your dad, eh?" he asked softly. "Listen, Jess. Did he ... did he ... ?"

I shook my head. "No. He'd never ... hit me. We just yelled."

"Sometimes the yelling's worse. With the other, it's over quick and that's that."

I could tell by the way he shrugged that he regretted saying anything. He dropped his hand.

"Listen, you don't have to come if you don't want to," he said.

163

I straightened my shoulders and managed a smile. "You can't get rid of me that easily. What are we waiting for?"

❦ ❦ ❦

Willow Creek Ranch, Alberta, 1908, July 16
After being settled in the saddle by Father, I waved to Madeline, who was standing on the veranda. Then I turned Phantom towards the hills.

Father laughed and called out, "Wait for me, Ian. Don't forget, you've been sick, dear fellow. Besides, we haven't decided where we'll go yet."

I shouted over my shoulder. "We can go 'bearing East and a quarter North' and maybe we can find a treasure!"

With that, to everyone's amazement I'm sure, and no less my own, Phantom and I made a run for the far hill, across the little stream and through the trees.

"Ian!" I could hear Father cry. "Ian. Wait!"

But I wouldn't stop. I was on the back of my Phantom horse, riding towards the sunlight.

CHAPTER 20

"HER NAME IS ALPHA," BEN SAID. "SHE'S A QUIET OLD thing."

I nodded, my tongue stuck to the roof of my mouth. It was like sitting on top of a moving mountain. She shifted under me, her long legs bending and straightening while my backside and hips tried to adjust to the dips and sways. Leather creaked with every movement.

Prue sat to one side, smiling up at us, eager to get going.

Standing with one hand on Alpha's neck, Ben gathered the reins in his other hand and said, "Okay. You cross these so that the left falls over her right shoulder and the right over her left. See? That way they join and you hold both at once."

I nodded, my brain in a turmoil.

"She's neck reined," he continued. "That means you pull the left one and she goes left. And vice versa. Like steering. Don't give her too many hard yanks or you'll confuse her. A gentle tug and she'll get the message. Most of the time, she'll just follow Bower and me. Okay?"

I tried to smile. My hands were gripping the reins so hard

I wasn't sure they'd ever open again.

He was laughing at me, I could tell. His lips weren't smiling, but there was a glitter in his eyes. I'd have to relax. But just as I loosened my knee-gripping hold, Alpha backed up a few steps and seemed to slip. I jerked on the reins and gasped, "She — she's falling."

Alpha must have sensed my panic, because she stood stock-still.

Ben swung himself up onto Bower. This time he *was* grinning.

I blushed. "Well, it felt like she was slipping."

"Horses have four legs. That's two more than you," he said. "She won't fall."

"Why did she back up? I — "

"You'd back up, too, if you'd been tied right up against a fence. Now, if *you* want her to back up, click your tongue and pull low and straight back. But when she's in forward and you want to stop her, you pull back on the reins and say 'whoa.' Loud and firm. She's listening." With a dry chuckle, he added, "If you could see your face. It's all eyes."

This was a Ben I hadn't seen before. Relaxed, grinning, eyes crinkled with laughter. He swung Bower around and headed towards a long trail that wound up through the pines. I pulled gently on Alpha's right rein and she carefully four-stepped into position, Prue in the rear.

Ben led the way along the edge of the wood until we came to a low creek filled with small rounded boulders and rocks. He looked back at me and said, "It's only about a foot deep — and Alpha could do it blindfolded — all the horses can."

"You go first, so I can watch Bower do it," I said shakily.

In two seconds Bower had tiptoed elegantly across. I let

the reins loosen. Alpha carefully plonked her way over and around the biggest rocks and in no time at all, we were beside them. I couldn't keep the idiotic grin off my face.

After that, I did relax. Well, to be honest, there were a couple of times when I figured it was all over, but Alpha knew what she was doing. The image of the man and horses outside the window kept sneaking into my mind, so I talked to Alpha a mile a minute to try and push it back out again. Now and then, she would bob her head up and down and let out a soft blowing snort—almost as if she was agreeing with all the nonsense I was babbling. Ben tended to get a little bit ahead, which was just as well, because I must have sounded like a gibbering fool.

About a mile from the ranch, we reached a grassy clearing. Ben swung Bower around and trotted back to me. "You want to keep going? It's really nice on the ridge above Broad Valley."

"Is it far? It won't get dark before we get back?"

He shook his head. "Nah. It's only about a mile. Percy says you can imagine the old homesteads that used to be up there. And he's right."

"Percy must know this area really well, huh?" I asked.

Ben nodded. "Someday I'm gonna be an outfitter. Percy and me—we got a deal. He says he'll help me, but first I've gotta finish grade twelve and one year of college." He pushed his hat up a bit. "He thinks I'll end up being a vet, but I don't know..." He hesitated. "He's gettin' old. I want us to get going on something together before it's too late."

He gazed towards the break of dark trees behind me. Sadness shadowed his face.

"Come on," he said gruffly. "Let's get going."

Slowly, we climbed higher and higher through the trees, the evening light falling across the wide path in stripes of warm yellow. About fifteen minutes later, we came out onto a wide sloping ridge overlooking a deep valley with open land down the middle and clutches of trees on either side. A lime-green hill rolled up towards us, and in the distance, the fields were every colour of blue and dark green. The sun lay lightly on the treetops, but the valley was in a cooling shadow. Beyond the ridge, thunderclouds were forming. It was domestic and wild, familiar and secret, all at the same time.

We watched a small herd of cattle move slowly across a fenced field.

"Look," said Ben, pointing.

I followed his finger and saw something moving in the field below us.

"What is it?"

"Coyote. After gophers, probably."

The small foxlike animal stood stock-still, his pointed face directed up at us.

"Good hearing, eh?" said Ben. "Look at him. Suspicious. Ranchers don't like coyotes. They go after chickens, even a sick calf."

"What's that?" I said, sitting up. "Do you hear it? Behind us. On the trail. Riders?"

Ben listened, his face quiet. "No, I don't hear anything, but let's get out of the way, just in case. Don't want the horses spooked."

Alpha and I followed him to a line of thick brush well clear of the ridge's edge.

"I don't think I hear it any more," I said.

"Where's that darn Prue? Gone off somewhere. There she is." He whistled. Prue didn't come. He whistled again.

"Darn it. Probably trailed a rabbit," he said. "I'll get her." He slid off Bower and disappeared into a wall of willow.

At the same moment, two riders crashed out of the bushes at the side of the trail. A thin small boy was riding ahead, his brown hair flying. Behind him rode a man, a fierce grin splitting his face. The boy slowed his horse and looked over his shoulder. When the man caught up, the boy spurred his horse again, his face alight. In a breath, both riders were past me, thundering down the hill, straight across the valley. Then, like a wash of water-colour across a wet page, they faded away into the evening light long before they reached the other side.

Ben appeared in front of me. I dragged my leg over the saddle and dropped shakily to the ground.

"Did you see them?" I grabbed his arm with both hands and held on tight. "Did you?"

He shook his head. "Who?"

"Two riders. A man and a boy. They rode down there."

He frowned and shook his head. "Couldn't have. Not down there."

I ran towards the spot where the riders had thundered down the steep incline.

"I saw them," I said. "They went right this way."

"It's way too steep. The trail goes along the ridge to the right. Besides, the grass isn't even trampled."

"They came out of the bushes, not along the trail," I said firmly. "And they galloped down there."

He gave me a curious look. "They musta been goin' pretty fast. I couldn't have been more than fifty feet away and I didn't hear anything."

I didn't care what he was saying. I knew what I had seen. The man was the same one in the yard saddling the horses. The boy had to be Ian Shaw.

I stared out over the valley. I had not imagined those riders. The man's wide grin, his billowing shirt, the boy's flying hair and excited face, the sweat on the flanks of their horses—it had all been real.

I jumped when Ben touched my arm.

"You okay?"

I nodded. Looking down that valley, I made myself a promise. I'd find out why they had returned to the ranch—why they'd left their own time and were now living in ours.

❦ ❦ ❦

Willow Creek Ranch, Alberta, 1908, July 16
I can still hear them. The horses' hooves pounding through the woods, up the hill and down onto the trail that led to the other side of the valley. I waited for Father, and he insisted that we stop to rest.

"We can have another quick race, along the ridge and down to the ranch later," he said firmly. "We have to think of the horses."

I nodded happily and allowed him to help me from the saddle. Gently he lowered me onto a shady spot thick with grass.

"Someday I'll be able to get down by myself," I said. "I'll strengthen my arms and my good leg. We can even strap a cane to the saddle. And I'll work hard. We can figure it out together. After she goes, of course. I'll work hard. I'll be a great help to you, Father. You'll see. We can buy one of those leg braces out of the catalogue so I'll be able to help you clear that wall of forest for more grazing. You may not have fit sons like Mr. Parks, but I'll work harder than the three of them put together. After she goes."

Father pulled a blade of grass carefully from its stalk

and chewed on the tender end. Then he said what I already knew. "She may not go. And she could make...life could be hard. I wouldn't want to see you give up again."

"I won't. Not if *you* stand up to her." I watched his face carefully. "Like you did the day she left with Mr. Eagleton. And by allowing this today."

He nodded and laughed. "She's not here today; that makes it easy. But, I'll try, Ian. I couldn't stand up to her before. I was afraid I'd lose you. Now I can see you intend to stay."

"I intend to stay," I said gravely.

He gazed out over the valley. "I don't know what I imagined ranching would be like," he said. "But this isn't it. Oh, I'd be happy enough on my own, but I should have given more thought to her. And to you. Poor little mite that you were. I fell for all the glamorous leaflets sent out by the government. Peaches on every tree, they said. Bring your finest clothes for the tea parties, they said. I was pretty stupid to believe them. That's why I can't fight her anger."

"She hates me," I said softly.

"She doesn't hate you, Ian. She loves you. Maybe too much. She's never been able to show her love the way others do. But at one time she — well, she was the kind of woman I'd always admired. She rode like a man. She danced like an angel. She took up nursing before we left, so she could do her duty as one of the great new Canadian landowners. I admired that."

He shook his head sadly. "Then, when we arrived, she found out that rich and poor, English and German, Irish and Ukrainian — we were *all* landowners. She was just the wife of an overworked homesteader."

I sighed and thought about that inflexible individual who had become my worst enemy, an enemy I hated and feared, and for a moment, I wavered. How bitterly she had been disappointed—first with me and then with her new life in Canada.

Could Father be right? Did that strange cold woman indeed love me? How could that be? Surely if you love someone, you don't punish them for your own unhappiness. It isn't loving someone that matters. It's what you *do* with that love. And she was destroying us all with hers.

"You're suddenly very quiet, old chap," Father said. "A penny for them?"

"I was just thinking that I have to get out from under—her love, if that is what this is," I said bitterly. "We both have to. Somehow. We'll have to face her together."

Father's eyes darkened and he looked away. Resting one forearm on each bent knee, he gazed at the ground. My heart went out to him. I know he is not a very strong man. Maybe not strong enough to win the final battle. I pray that I am.

"Come on, Father," I said brightly. "We've still got a race to finish."

He looked up and smiled, some of the pain leaving his face. "Righto. And this time I won't let you win. I'm out for blood, so take care!"

I laughed as Father placed me securely in the saddle. Phantom shifted with impatience. At the sound of Father's "Go!" we were off.

Father and Lally came in just a little ahead of us. I am

very tired tonight—with that wonderful weariness that comes from a full day outside. Father has promised that we shall go riding tomorrow. And I have warned him that Phantom and I will really give him a run for his money. Hurry tomorrow!

CHAPTER 21

A S WE WALKED INTO THE RANCH HOUSE, A LOW
mutter of thunder told us we'd made it home just
in time. The kitchen was tidy, tea towels drying
over the wooden rack on the counter.

I poked my head around the parlour door. Dad was
slouched in front of the cold fireplace, legs stretched
straight out, shoulders low in the chair — staring into the
pile of half-burnt logs and grey ashes. I could smell whisky.

I cleared my throat. He glanced over, then back at the
fireplace. "I've been riding," I said. "Happy now?"

He didn't notice the sarcasm, just nodded and grunted,
"Good."

"Did you talk to Mom?"

He took a gulp from the glass and lowered his arm,
slopping liquid over his hand and the chair. "I was up there
half an hour ago. She wouldn't let me in." His words were
thick, slurred.

"Did you actually talk to her?"

"Yeah. Through the bloody door. Said she was tired.
Took two of those pills the doctor gave 'er. Or so she said. I

gotta talk to her. She shoulda let me in."

Struggling to his feet, he drained his glass. "I'm goin' ta bed." He stared, as if looking for something in my face, then shrugged loosely and staggered forward a few steps. "All the time. Round and round. I'm tired of — " he pointed, but missed his head by six inches " — tired of thinking. She should...she should talk ta me. I didn't mean — it was supposed to... "

His voice trailed off. He turned, put his glass on the mantle with a clatter and walked a crooked line towards the front stairway. I should have felt sorry, I suppose, but the sight of him staggering off like a backstreet drunk disgusted me.

"Very mature, Father Dear," I muttered.

"Hey, Jess, you want a sandwich?" Ben asked from the kitchen. "I'll make you my all-time super-sub. But without the sub. No buns."

He'd practically emptied the fridge. He was smearing butter and mayonnaise and mustard, and piling cold meats, cheeses, pickles, thick slices of tomatoes and whole lettuce leaves on doorstops of bread. Then he pressed a second doorstop on top of each sandwich and gave me one. I examined it as if I'd been handed something from outer space, while he waited, hands on hips. Up to that moment, I wasn't hungry. Now, the smell made my mouth water.

"Good thing I didn't eat much supper," I said, before wrapping my mouth around one corner. Mayonnaise and tomato juice dripped on the table. Mom's face, with its lost eyes and pale cheeks, forced its way into my mind. I pushed it away. I wanted to forget everything — just for a few minutes.

"How about a Coke?" Ben asked, plunking a fizzing glass in front of me. "Just like in a country restaurant. No ice. Now you can make ladylike burps all through the meal."

I had just taken another bite and burst out laughing, covering my mouth just in time. Ben guffawed loudly, his eyes scrunched up, his cheeks creased with long dimples. My heart did that funny tilt again.

We sat across from each other, chewing and laughing and guzzling Coke. Ben turned on the radio. I had it set to a light-rock station, but he gave me a look of mock contempt and spun the dial until he found a fast-paced fiddle-backed song about trucking along the highway.

We talked about school. In the fall, I'd be bussed about thirty-five miles to the same comprehensive high school he went to. We were both going into grade twelve. He was taking mostly sciences, on Winny's advice.

"Will you go back home to live?" I asked. His face hardened. "Sorry. None of my business."

He shrugged. "I'll figure it out before summer's over."

I could have kicked myself. The radio station was advertising stone-washed jeans. Our silence continued through a loud Ricky Skaggs down-home song.

Finally Ben said, "You seen Winny and Percy's place yet?" I shook my head. "It's really nice. A little yellow wood house. With a creek running right behind it. The neighbours feed the chickens when they're working here. They lay the biggest brown eggs you've ever seen."

I pretended to gawk. "The neighbours lay big brown eggs? I'd like to meet them."

"Them? Or their eggs?" he asked, and we both spluttered into our Cokes, more from relief than from our feeble wit.

At that moment, a sad song came on the radio. The sweet breathy tone of a harmonica sent an eerie tickle up my spine.

"I have that tape," said Ben. He reached into his pocket, pulled out a silver and red harmonica and, cupping his hands around it, began to play along with the music.

The hair on my arms lifted. He played the harmonica! He and the musician on the radio blended perfectly. Sometimes it sounded as if only one person was playing. When it was done and the loud-mouthed announcer returned, Ben put the harmonica back in his pocket, shrugging sheepishly. A swell of thunder thudded in the distance. The radio squawked once before becoming a wash of crackly static.

"Jeez, I didn't think you were that bad," I said.

His face was tinged with pink, but he smiled. It was the closest I could come to telling him how great he could play.

"Did you play that thing when you were riding over here the other morning?" I asked casually.

He frowned. "No. Why?"

I felt queasy. "I thought I heard it. Or something like it. And both Mom and I heard it the night you and Dad were camping. I wonder if — "

No. I couldn't talk about it. He'd think I was as nutty as Mom. My heart took a nose-dive. Mom. I shouldn't have walked out on her. I'd have to apologize tomorrow.

Ben said quietly, "Your mom's been pretty sick, eh?"

I nodded. "Yeah."

"Your brother dying like that...it musta been hard. I — well — I almost died once."

"Really?"

"Two days before my twelfth birthday. Car accident. My parents died. I didn't."

"That's when you came to live with your grandfather?"

He nodded. "Yeah. Sometimes, I think the old man wishes I'd died in the crash, too."

I sat up. "You're kidding, right?"

"Not really. Percy says my grampa was really proud of my dad. Dad was pretty good-looking. Hard to believe when you see the rest of us, eh? My Gramma Hodge was pretty. I've seen pictures. She died when my dad was a kid.

"Dad was really smart in school. Grampa let him go to university — so he'd come back and help expand the business. Maybe open a farm-machinery lot. But my dad didn't come back. He got married and became an engineer for a big oil company. Grampa howled blue murder. Said he hadn't sent him to some fancy school so that he could go work for someone else. But Percy says the real reason he was mad was because he missed Dad."

"And then your dad was killed," I breathed.

"Yeah. They hadn't talked for years. And then Grampa sent a letter asking Dad to come see him. We were driving back here for Christmas and bam! a gravel truck ran right into us. My mom and dad were killed outright. I was asleep in the back seat with a seat belt on. I didn't have a scratch."

"And he's held that against you all these years?"

"I figure he blames himself more. He wasn't too bad at first. He was tough, but he let me come and go to school, work around the garage and that." He stopped.

"And then?" I urged.

I guess something in my face told him it was okay.

He shrugged nonchalantly. "I was a pretty small kid, but I was tough. When I was about thirteen, I started hanging out with Percy. Riding and stuff. That's when the old man started slamming me around a bit, but only when he was drunk." Ben tousled Prue's ears. "I got used to staying out of his way. Sometimes, when he'd been drinking all night, he'd drag me out of bed. It could be pretty bad. But then I started growing. Fast." He laughed, a short dry sound in the air. A growl of thunder answered it.

178

My heart was pounding hard in my throat. How could he sound so matter-of-fact? "Why didn't you tell someone?"

"I did. Once. It was a dumb thing to do. I told Percy. Him and Winny went to see Grampa." His mouth thinned. "You shoulda seen the lambasting I got *that* night. Afterwards, he tried to make me quit school. But I wasn't old enough."

"Could you talk to your friends?"

He smiled again, a sad, adult smile. "Who's gonna be friends with someone who can't have anyone over after school because he's gotta work at the family gas station? And who has a drunk for a grandfather. All I had were Nosy-Parker social workers."

"Couldn't they do anything?" I asked.

His face tightened. "I wouldn't tell them. Telling Percy that time was a big mistake, believe me. I can handle the old man on my own. So I told Percy to back off. Him and Winny."

"Don't you hate your grandfather?"

"No. It wasn't my fault Dad died. But I still felt guilty. And it was almost as if the old man'd been...you know, betrayed. Sometimes, *most* of the time, he called me Tim — my dad's name — when he was...like that. The next day he'd put his hand on my shoulder, so I knew he was sorry. He never used his fists. Only his open hand. Most of the time he was hitting my dad, not me — which was funny because Emmet says the old man never hit my dad when they were growing up."

"Ben! You're giving him excuses!"

He shook his head. "No. I just know him. Uncle Emmet kinda looked out for me when he lived with us. Last winter he moved in with his girlfriend, Rosie. Once when Grampa was really plastered — at Christmas — he started in on me — in front of Uncle Emmet and Rosie." He smiled in remembrance — a crooked sliver of bitterness. "Big mistake. Emmet stepped in and took the next hit. The old man hurt his shoulder. Hitting my uncle musta been like hitting a steel door."

I remembered the younger man waiting by the tow truck and knew exactly what Ben meant.

"Why don't you move in with your uncle?"

"He asked me to. After Christmas. But Rosie's got two little kids and they're really crowded in that puny trailer. And I couldn't leave the old man. At least, not then."

"Something changed."

He nodded. "The day I started here, I told him I was going to college after graduation. He didn't say a word. Just hauled off and socked me one. He's been real sick the past few months so it wasn't much of a punch. But he was stone-cold sober. He'd never done that before. I shoved a few things in my saddle-bags and came here."

I reached out and touched his sleeve with my fingertips. He groped for my hand and together we sat, lost in our own thoughts. Mine tumbled over one another — Scotty and Mom, Ian Shaw and his mother Augusta, and Ben, whose warm hand gripped mine as if he would never let it go.

CHAPTER 22

"JESS?"

I looked up, realizing I'd been staring at my clenched fists. I couldn't even remember Ben letting go of my hand. The table was cleared and Ben was wiping it with a wet cloth.

"You okay, Jess? You were looking..."

"Yeah, I'm okay." I took a deep breath. "Listen, I've got to clear out that room next to my mom's. It's jammed with Mrs. Parks' stuff and ours, all mixed together. Could you give me a hand with it tomorrow? There's something I—I need from there. And it's such a mess I'll need some help moving stuff around."

He looked pleased. "Sure. If Percy lets me have some time off."

I nodded. He stood by the sink, looking awkward, as if unsure what to do next.

"Listen..." he said, "about all that...uh..."

"I won't blab it around," I said. "Maybe one day I'll tell you about the mess we're in here." I knew there was no way to compare our lives—but I think he understood.

"Well," he said. "I guess I'll see you in the morning. Do you need me to help close up?"

"Thanks, I'm okay. I'll do it."

He hesitated, then said, "Okay... I'll see you tomorrow."

When he was gone, I sat trying to fit together all the jagged pieces in my head — to begin at the beginning of all that had happened and work my way through to where I was now. But the pieces kept scattering and I lost track of where I was. Ben came into those thoughts pretty often, his smooth angular face, with its straight nose and dark eyes. I should have asked him to stay a bit longer — I was hopeless. Still, there was tomorrow.

Finally, I gave up, scraped back my chair and walked slowly through the parlour. A lamp stood on a little table by the door into the dining room. Its light softly glanced off the varnish of the tables and chairs, outlining the old fieldstone fireplace and reflecting dimly off the brass bits and other ornamental tack hanging above the mantle. The corners of the room were clogged with shadow, and the night pressed against the window-panes like black velvet.

I realized with a funny jolt that the dining room must have been the living area of the original homestead, with the veranda for summer use. The T.V. room behind the dining room had probably been the kitchen. Directly above were the three small bedrooms, one of them Mom's... and Ian Shaw's.

I stood very still, chin up and eyes narrowed. Something wasn't right. A now-familiar sense of foreboding was filling the air. There was not a sound outside or in. Suddenly, very close, came the deep quick cough of thunder. A flash of lightning followed, bathing everything in a strange white radiance. No. It couldn't be! A clap of thunder overhead rattled the house. I felt it through the soles of my boots.

Then another flash of light and another thud-crash. The second flash confirmed what I had seen — a figure, standing at the veranda door, looking in.

Rolling my back around the doorjamb, I stood pressed against the parlour wall. The smell of rain and musty wet wood seemed to rise up around me. The little light was out — the power lines must have been hit. Could I make a run for it without crashing into furniture and alerting her? For it *was* her. The black and white woman. Augusta Shaw.

Another thunder bomb dropped straight onto the house, and I was sure it would split the roof in two. From the open door, a cold rush of wind swirled through the house, rattling the lampshades. Beside me, a window was also open. Curtains billowed in, touching me like cold damp fingers. All at once, a plaintive sound drifted in on the wind and sighed back out the window. It was the thin whistle of the harmonica — its tones coming and going like sorrowful breathing, full of sadness and yearning.

Please, please, let it be Ben, my brain cried silently. But I knew it wasn't. Outside, rain pounded straight into the ground. I heard the veranda screen door open slowly. Now, the music seemed to be coming from inside the house, faint and eerie against the wash of the downpour.

I had to look. Peering cautiously around the corner, I saw the pale glow of her hair and dress just inside the door. The fabric shimmered in the darkness, creating its own pale light. Something was very wrong. She was bent over, one arm clutching her side, the shimmering hair loose and straggly over her shoulders. She moved forward in uneven strides, the dark face tilted up and to the side. She could hear the music, too. She stumbled towards the front stairs.

By the time I reached the bottom of the narrow staircase, the glimmering skirt was moving slowly towards the turning at the top. I followed, one nervous step at a time, terrified that she might start down again and I'd have to face her.

When I reached the bend, my heart was making such a racket it took me a few seconds to realize that the music had stopped again.

I stuck my head cautiously around the doorframe. She was in front of Mom's room, leaning against the door, doubled over, as if in pain. How had she hurt herself? What had happened? Where was Ian?

Something else caught my attention—someone, another dark figure, was in the hallway. The boy? The shadowy form straightened and moved forward. A man! Ian's father? The woman didn't seem aware of him.

A low moan echoed along the narrow space. It came from the man in the shadows. The moan was followed by a gulping sob. Suddenly, the tall figure lurched towards Mom's door and passed right through Augusta Shaw as if she wasn't there. I had to hold down a hysterical giggle. Of course she wasn't there. No one was really there. I probably wasn't here, either.

"I'm sorry, love," a voice said. "Open the door, Jeanie. Please. We...we've gotta talk. I—I miss you, Jeanie. We gotta work this out. I—I—" The voice broke.

Dad! I edged around the corner and pressed close to the box room door, groping for the door handle. He mustn't see me. It would be too awful.

"Jeanie? Honey? Can you wake up?" Dad begged, his words thick with sorrow and booze.

He lurched backwards and slammed against the wall. The woman remained unaware of him. Dad's long figure slumped down until he was sitting on the floor. He cried out—a terrible sound I'd never heard before. Suddenly, the woman straightened, her body signalling alarm. Had she heard Dad? All at once, another cry lifted and turned into a strange keening wail. I almost bit through my lip. That wasn't Dad. That was *her*.

"Eeeen! Eeen!" came the thin call. Up and up it went in register, swirling around the hall and then dying slowly.

I backed into the box room, leaving the door open a crack. Everything was very quiet. When I nervously peeked through the gap, I saw something that made my scalp crawl with terror. Augusta was floating towards me, her white hair streaming out behind. Suddenly, she staggered, and as she reached out for the wall, she lifted her head and looked straight at me. A ghastly shriek, riding on a blast of freezing wind, threw me backwards.

Darkness twisted and whirled. Half falling onto a box, I put my head between my knees. When everything finally stopped turning, I sat up, very slowly. The door was open. The hall was dark. She was gone.

I sucked in a loud ragged breath. I couldn't make a run for it. I couldn't pass Dad in the hall. I didn't even dare turn a light on, in case he saw it. So I sat on the box and waited, hoping *She* wouldn't return and *He* would soon go to bed.

As the minutes ticked by, however, my seething mind slowed down. With Augusta's strong spirit gone for the present, I found myself concentrating on Dad. I didn't know what to think about him now. I didn't know what to think about anything any more. I closed my eyes and saw Mom and Dad and me alone on our separate islands—close enough to see each other, but not close enough to touch. Would we be able to move together again? I sat and thought about it for a long time. When I peered down the hall, Dad was gone.

185

CHAPTER 23

B Y THE TIME I'D DRAGGED MYSELF OUT OF BED AND downstairs, it was almost nine o'clock. Winny looked me over, her lips pressed tight.

"Has His Highness decided to have a little lie-in this morning, too?" she asked. "And where is Ben?"

I gave her a dazed look and a shrug.

She humphed and put bacon and eggs in front of me. I was just pouring myself a glass of orange juice when the pathetic remains of my father stumbled into the room.

"What time is it?" he mumbled. "My clock stopped during the storm last night. And I stepped on my watch in the dark. Must have the flu. Don't feel well."

Ben wandered in right behind. "Sorry, Winny. My clock was off."

"Hmph. Electric clocks. Percy and I can't use *our* clocks as an excuse."

"Unless you forget to wind them." Ben grinned.

"We *have* heard of batteries, Mr. Smartypants," Winny snapped. "Sit down and eat."

Behind their backs, Ben held his nose and pointed up

the stairs. Then he pointed at Dad. Great. Dad must have made a mess in the bathroom. Suddenly bacon and eggs didn't seem very appetizing. It appeared that Dad agreed. He went a chalky green and staggered down the hall to the downstairs bathroom.

"Hmph," said Winny. "So that explains the glass and empty bottle in the parlour. Well, all I can say is he'd better clean his own mess up. I'm not doing it."

I didn't say anything. After Scotty died, Dad and I'd managed to keep the house reasonably clean, but he never cooked a meal and was definitely a household-chauv type. Something told me he would expect the "hired help" to clean up after him.

"Does he do this often?" Winny asked.

I shook my head. "Never. He doesn't drink much at all. But last night—he—well..."

She nodded.

Ben said, "I'll clean the bathroom. I already did the worst of it. Jeez, he was sick everywhere."

Winny grinned. "You were about to get a good talking-to, but I forgive you. Percy's already done half the chores while the able-bodied help," she included me in her beetling glance, "was still sawing logs."

Ben grabbed two pieces of toast and headed for the door. "I'll clean the rest of the mess when I'm done out here. Then I'll come and get you, Jess."

"Hold it right there, bucko," Winny snapped. "Take Percy his coffee. Here." She handed Ben a big steaming tin cup. "The boss and Percy were supposed to go over to Crawford's place to buy a horse, but *someone* isn't going to be up to it, so you'll have to go instead. It'll take you most of the morning. Then—"

Ben interrupted her. "I can't. I promised Jess I'd—"

"It's okay," I interrupted. "He—he was going to help me move that stuff around in the box room. But I can leave the big stuff for later."

"Are you sure?" he asked. "Maybe you should—you know—wait a bit."

I felt myself growing warm under Winny's gaze. "I'm sure, thanks." I began clearing the table.

Ben stepped back and stumbled over the doorstop. His face a bright red, he checked the level in the coffee cup. "I'll—I'll see you later," he said, and hurried away.

"You two seem to be getting along okay, huh?" Winny said nonchalantly, but there was teasing in her voice.

I turned to glare at her and found her grinning widely. I changed my face to look like I didn't care and made a lot of noise clattering plates.

"I'm taking your mom to my place this morning," she said, while we did the dishes. "Looks like a nice day building after all that rain. I thought we'd sit outside and have some iced tea. I need to check my garden, weed a bit, cut some flowers for here. Brighten this place up a bit. You want to come?"

I shook my head. "I'll get some sorting done in the box room. By myself."

She leaned over and, with her hands in suds, pushed me with her big shoulder. I pushed her back. Then we spluttered with laughter.

Dad edged into the room and we spluttered louder. His colour was fish-belly grey. Winny dried her hands, poured a cup of black coffee and handed it to him. He drank it almost in one swallow, steam and all, and held his cup out for more.

"Can't eat," he muttered. "I'll—I'll just go out and give the guys a hand. I gotta pay that Crawford fella for that horse. Haven't had the flu in years." He took his hat off the peg and put it gingerly on his head. When the screen door slapped shut behind him, he flinched as if he'd been shot in the stomach. I smiled to myself. Was I actually feeling sorry for my father?

"I hope Ben and Percy don't let him sit in the middle," I giggled.

"I'm just glad I don't have to go along," Winny said. "I'll go get your mom and we'll see you later, eh? You'll have to come and see our place soon, though."

"Next time," I said. "Right now I want to clear through that junk in the box room. There's some things of mine I've been looking for — that haven't been unpacked yet."

I wished that were true. The things I needed to find didn't even belong to me. They belonged to three restless spirits from another time.

An hour later, I watched our car, with Winny driving and Mom as passenger, roll down the road. Percy's blue truck was gone, too. Only a few horses cropped their way slowly along the fence. The air was still and the sun sifted lazily into the box room. I was alone.

I tried not to notice the brooding sadness that seemed to have fallen around the house. I gathered up the hatbox and its contents and left the room as fast as I could.

I sat cross-legged on my unmade bed, looking into the round box. I reached in and picked up a large sheet of cardboardy paper folded in four. It was a soft pastel certificate bordered with pink and white roses, recording the marriage of Augusta Louisa Kittering and Nigel Chipperfield Shaw. They had been "joined in Holy Wedlock" in Canterbury, Kent, England, in 1894.

I reached in again and came up with a brown envelope. Inside were two brownish photographs mounted on hard-

189

board. The first was the ranch house as it must have looked shortly after being built — the veranda straight and true, the foundation firm. There were no trees around it then. It stood stark and plain, the sepia colour giving it a distant, almost worn look despite its spruce newness. It was just as I had seen it yesterday — except then it had been in full colour.

The next picture was like a quick electric shock. There they were — all three of them.

They were on the steps of the veranda, the boy seated on the bottom stair, one leg thrust out in front, a smaller leg tucked behind, a pair of oddly shaped canes on either side of him. The man stood on the middle step, the woman on the top.

The man had his hands in his pockets. He wore a collarless shirt buttoned to his neck and a dark vest and pants. His hair had been plastered down, but a bit had fallen loose and hung over his forehead. He was smiling, his chin tucked in a little. He looked shy or perhaps embarrassed.

The boy was thin and small, dressed in a plain shirt and dusty greyish pants. He was also smiling, with exactly the same shy look as his father, but his back was ramrod straight and I had a feeling that he had an eagerness, a toughness, that ran deep.

They were the ones I'd seen riding wildly along the ridge. My eyes skimmed back and forth between Ian and Nigel Shaw trying to avoid even the edge of the woman's dark dress.

Then, slowly, I let my eyes travel up the skirt. The long thin hands were pressed to her waist, the fingers tightly entwined. The bodice of the dress had furls of lace down the front, with sleeves puffed at the shoulder and narrow at the wrist. At the collar was a large oval brooch. Her neck was long and slender. I glanced away, then summoning courage, I looked her square in the face.

There she was. Augusta Shaw. Her black hair was drawn back from a smooth wide forehead. The eyebrows were thin and arched, the nose long with delicate nostrils. The mouth was tight. She was frowning slightly against the bright light behind the photographer, and in each small shadow under the brows, there was only a faint shaping of the eyes.

Seeing her so restrained, so rigid, so unsmiling — standing on the steps of the very house I was sitting in, the past and the present became blurred. Would these figures in the photo begin to breathe — to move?

I turned it over quickly. Someone had written in brown ink in a careful copperplate writing, "The Shaw Family — On their veranda, taken by John Parks, May, 1908."

An overwhelming sadness washed through me. If Percy and Lettice were right, the boy and the young woman could soon be dead. Was the shy man smiling into the camera about to have his world turned upside-down? How soon, after this picture was taken, had it happened?

I dug through the rest of the stuff, but most of it was legal papers and bills of cattle purchases and lists of supplies. My hand touched something cold right near the bottom. A small silver and red harmonica. So that's where the music had come from. Ian. It was lying on top of a thin scribbler. I lifted the little book out and flipped it open to the first page — it was crowded with lines and lines of small, tight writing. It began, "I, Ian Shaw, have decided to begin another account of the events in this house ... "

CHAPTER 24

"FATHER HAS PROMISED THAT WE SHALL GO RIDING tomorrow. And I have warned him that Phantom and I will really give him a run for his money. Hurry tomorrow!"

I lay staring at the ceiling for a long time. The weight of sadness had grown so heavy it was difficult to breathe. Had tomorrow come for Ian? Why had his journal ended so abruptly that summer day in 1908? When had his mother returned? Lettice had said that *She* had died, too. Had she come back from her trip carrying an infectious illness?

I would never know. There were no answers to those questions. I had come as far as I could. Ian's journal ended smack in the middle of a terrible conflict with *Her*, and I would never know the results. Frustration raged through me. Would she keep haunting us? What did each of them want from us—or from one another? I wasn't even sure why Augusta Shaw was walking the halls. The logical answer seemed to be that Ian had locked her out. But what about the last time I'd seen her—with her hair spilling over her shoulders and her wild screams? Eeen! Eeen! It came to me then—that's what she was calling: Ian! Ian!

And those screams weren't angry—they were a mix of fear and shock and grief. The same sounds my mother made when the police told her about Scotty. I felt a grim satisfaction knowing that Augusta Shaw had suffered. I was glad that she was unhappy.

I smoothed my hand over the cover of the journal. How had it ended up in the hatbox? Who had discovered it behind the wall? More than likely it was the Parks family, when they insulated the house years later. Unless *She* had found it.

Anger, like dust, caught in my throat. It was so unfair! Ian had nothing of his own—except this secret journal—until Phantom came into his life. I hated *Her*, with her vicious tongue and her mean spirit. Something slammed into my mind. What—what if she had found out about Phantom? No! She couldn't. Ian and Nigel were so careful. But she was clever—and wicked.

"Did you find out? Did you ruin that, too?" I cried, glaring at the tall woman standing on the steps in the brown long-ago light. "Why couldn't you leave him alone? I hate you, Augusta Shaw! I hate you!"

Behind me the door swung shut with a loud crack. My body jolted and my teeth snapped together. Pain seared through my tongue. In a blind fury, I ran to the door and hammered on it.

"You don't scare me, Augusta Shaw. I'm not afraid of you!" I kicked the door for good measure and sat down on the edge of the bed, trembling and trying to nurse my bitten tongue. Tears of anger and pain seared my cheeks.

Slowly, the reality of what had happened seeped in. Alarmed, I crept to the door and turned the key in the lock. Then I packed everything into the hatbox, putting the harmonica, the photos and the journal on top. I pressed down the battered lid.

"Poor Ian," I whimpered. "It's just not fair. Poor, poor Ian. Why did you have to die? Why couldn't you grow up and help your dad and ride Phantom and...and..."

Scotty's face filled my mind. What had he wanted to do when he grew up? I'd never asked him. I choked back a sob. We'd had our whole lives to ask questions like that. Or so I thought. Did Ian know he would never grow up? Did Scotty?

I can't explain what happened then. It was as if Scotty spoke to me. I didn't hear his voice. But inside I felt myself changing. Not becoming happier or sadder, but something new and strange — a fierce, yet almost tender awareness of a different way of being, a feeling of light and space. With it came an understanding that Scotty was all right — and that I was going to make it through this.

I dug around in my bureau until I found Scotty's soccer shirt. I pulled it on and lay down on the bed. I didn't cry. What had happened was too big for tears. But I knew I would always miss him, and I would have to fill up that empty place with our good and bad times, our fights and our teasing. I'd find photos of him and put them in my room. He was still my kid brother.

I fell asleep, remembering our last picnic together. I'd taught Scotty to dive for stones wrapped in silver foil. He'd stopped being afraid of the water that day.

CHAPTER 25

A FEW HOURS LATER I WAS JOLTED AWAKE BY THE blaring of a horn. Sleepily, I stumbled to the window. Percy's old truck banged and clattered into the yard, churning up dust and stones. He was driving like Winny. Something was very wrong.

The driver's door screeched open and Percy jumped stiffly out of the truck, shouting, "Winny! Winny!"

The back door slammed and Winny came hurrying into view. "What are you shouting about, I—"

"Good, you're back. It's that damn Hodge. I seen him burnin' rubber on Highway Six and outdrove him here," he puffed. "He's not far behind. Saw his dust half a mile back."

I made it to the kitchen just as the tow truck rumbled to a grinding stop beside Percy's truck. Winny was alone, standing near the door.

"It's Ben's grampa," she said. "Percy's going to try and put him off."

"But we've got to warn Ben!" I cried. "The old man won't leave without seeing Ben!"

For a moment, I thought the unflappable Winny Eldridge was going to panic, but she took a deep breath, held up both hands and said calmly, "Don't worry, Jess. We'll handle this."

Mr. Hodge walked heavily into the room, his boots scraping the wood floor. He wore ancient denims and a stained white shirt. A big buckled belt, the kind rodeo riders wear, looked out of place against his gaunt frame. His small eyes cast around the room. Percy came limping in behind, looking anxiously for Ben.

Winny took the metal coffee pot off the stove and slammed it on the table. Mr. Hodge stared at her.

She spoke quietly in her deep voice. "I am *not* having any upset in this house."

Percy nodded and took off his hat. His rug sat firmly squared on his head. "There was no keepin' him out, Winny."

Winny eyeballed Mr. Hodge. "If you've come to talk, we'll listen. But if you so much as raise your voice, I'll call the police. Got it?"

"Where's my boy?" demanded the old man, his jowls wobbling. "I gotta talk to Ben. Alone."

"You'll come into the dining room," Winny said. "It's quieter there. Won't bother the Missus. Jess can get Ben. He's upstairs."

I was glad to leave them with Mr. Hodge. I ran upstairs and peered into Ben's room. He was sound asleep, snoring softly.

"Ben?" I whispered, shaking his arm.

"Wha—?" He blinked around and when he focused on my face, his smile was sleepy and sweet.

"Get up!" I said, poking him. "Percy and Winny want you downstairs. Didn't you hear the trucks?"

He stretched. "No. When we got back, I cleaned the bathroom and made my bed. I guess I zonked out." Suddenly he looked alert. "Trucks? What trucks?" He rolled over and looked out the window, then swung his feet to the floor. "The old man's here? Damn it! Is Percy with him?"

I managed to grab hold of him halfway down the stairs. "Ben. Please." The words choked out.

He stopped and I held on tightly to a handful of shirtsleeve. He leaned back against the wall. "The old man needs me, you know. What am I gonna do, Jess?"

I chewed my lip and studied his face. He looked defeated. He reached out with one hand. It ran up my neck and through my hair and pulled me close. I buried my face in his chest. He smelled like soap and salty sweat.

"I just can't leave him," he whispered.

I pulled away and stood with my back against the cold wall. "Yes!" I said loudly, then lowered my voice. "Yes, you can."

He looked at me, his mouth grim.

"Look, maybe he's sorry for what he's done to you," I said. "Maybe in a funny way, he's hoping to make it up to you before he dies. But *Ben*...he had six years to make you a home. He was so filled with hatred...and failure— he ended up *punishing* you all those years!"

Ben shook his head back and forth.

"What more do you owe him?" I continued urgently. "You've got a family—heck, *two* families—that would treat you way better than he would. Don't you see?"

He wrapped his arms across his chest tightly, the muscles in his forearms corded and hard under the skin. I touched his hand, but he pulled away. Doubling up, he slowly lowered himself onto the stairs.

Finally, his head lifted. He stared ahead, lost in thought. I pretended not to see him wipe his face with both hands.

"I'll talk to you later," he said, clumping down the stairs.

I followed and waited in the kitchen, watching them through the French doors into the dining room. Ben and his grandfather sat side by side, never once looking at each other. First Ben talked and then the old man. Their voices remained low. Now and again, Ben looked up and I knew Winny or Percy was saying something. A few times he nodded. The old man never looked away from his hands folded on the table.

Finally, everyone stood up. Ben said something to his grandfather, shrugging and looking worried at the same time. The old man reached out to support himself on the back of a chair. For just a fraction of a second, his other arm came up and hung in the air above Ben's shoulder, as if he was about to touch him. But then, the arm dropped and Ben stepped back.

Mr. Hodge pivoted on his heel and headed for the kitchen. The strain that was visible on his face from across the room was overpowering close up. I looked away, upset and confused by what I saw in those milky eyes.

He stopped, one hand on the door. "You'll come and see me."

"Yeah, sure, I'll come by. I still gotta get my things," said Ben in a low voice. "I'll come by."

The old man nodded and pushed through the door. When the tow truck's roar had died away, Ben looked at me. I didn't say anything; my heart was aching for him. I walked out of the house.

Crossing the yard, I dropped down beside the wall of the tack shed, in the shade, and leaned against the cooling logs. I knew Percy and Winny needed a few minutes to talk to Ben, but I also knew that he would come and sit beside me.

And he did — about fifteen minutes later. With an exhausted sigh, he pressed his head against the logs. We didn't talk, but held hands and listened to the sounds around us — the buzz of horseflies, the distant twitter of birds, the clatter of dishes inside the house.

A few minutes later, Winny and Percy walked through the back door, heading towards the small cabins. They each raised a hand and we waved back.

"They're going to rest," Ben said. "Winny ordered Percy to go, but he wouldn't unless she went with him."

"I'll go in and help her when she gets up," I said.

He sighed. "Jeez. That — that was..."

"I know."

"Grampa's sick."

"Yes."

"But, you know, when I sat on the stairs, I thought about Percy. He's getting older, too, and needs help around here and his place. I'd — well — I want to help him. Him and Winny."

"That's good."

"But I'll visit the old man. Uncle Emmet's been trying to fix up the garage, and Grampa's been fighting it every step of the way. Maybe now he'll listen. Emmet won't desert him," he said bitterly.

"You're not deserting anyone. Your uncle's there to keep an eye on him. You'll visit, like you said."

"Yeah, but I feel so —" He stopped.

Dad was coming towards us from the stables.

"Ben," he called. "I want to take a better look at that new horse. I'll need your help."

"See you later," Ben muttered.

I squeezed his hand and he looked startled, as if I'd said something really important. Then his whole face lit up.

CHAPTER 26

I PERCHED ON THE EDGE OF MOM'S BED, PULLED OUT Ian's journal and began to read. It didn't take long. The last words of the last entry hung in the air. Mom stared out the window, her hands clenched in her lap.

She was still wearing the cotton flowered dress she'd worn to Winny's and there was a dusting of sun-colour on her pale arms and the tip of her nose.

I handed her the journal, the two photographs and Ian's harmonica. She hardly looked at the stuff before thrusting it all back into my hands with a hard jerking motion. I blathered on, telling her everything: the face at the window, Augusta's night-time visits in the hallway outside her room, the strange man I'd seen saddling the horses, and the riders on the ridge overlooking the valley. The only thing I kept quiet about was Dad's drunken visit the night before.

When she turned to me, I saw something strange in her eyes — something I hadn't expected. Cold anger. Her voice was thin and tight. "Why are you doing this, Jess? Why are you insisting that this story has something — some bearing on my... my life — on Scotty's death?"

My face burned hot. "I'm not making this up, if that's what you mean!"

"I don't know what you're doing," she said wearily. "I know you feel you haven't been paid enough attention, Jess. And yes, I thought I was seeing Scotty. I know I'm sick and need help. But you're searching for answers that don't help me. It's as if you are deliberately punishing me."

I jumped up. The journal landed at her feet, the pictures and harmonica in her lap.

"Punishing you! Of course! *That's* what I've been doing all these weeks. I haven't tried to help you at all, have I? After all, I don't miss Scotty, do I? And Dad doesn't miss Scotty, either. Oh, no! Jeanie Locke is the only one suffering. *She's* the only one who misses Scotty," I sneered. "You've wrapped yourself in your Tragic Queen's Cloak. Everyone tiptoes around you. Winny calls Dad Your Highness, but it fits you better!"

"Listen here, Jess —" She was standing up now, her neck and face an angry mottled red.

"Everything I told you about the Shaws and everything I saw is true. I'm not lying!" I shouted, tears burning my eyes.

She was alarmed now. "Calm down, Jess," she said, "I —"

"You want to crack up and go under?" I cried. "Be my guest. Go ahead — wallow in it. You want to divorce Dad? Fine. *You* can wander around here like the Bride of Frankenstein. And Dad can race around like all three Stooges rolled into one. *I don't care!* I've had it with both of you. I can't make it better. I can't make us happy again." My voice broke. "Scotty isn't wandering around looking for you, Mom. He's dead. I miss him and I'm sorry, but I'm the one who's left. Okay? I'm alive and I'm here! You and Dad can suffer all you want. I've had enough!"

I stumbled through the door, slammed it behind me and stood on the other side — unable to move.

The door creaked open. "Jess?" Mom said in a small voice. "Come back inside. Please?"

"What's the point?" I muttered.

"Please, Jess?" Her eyes searched my face.

Reluctantly, I followed her into the room, perched on the edge of the bed, and stared at the plank floor. When the silence lengthened into minutes, I glanced up.

"I'm sorry, Jess," she said quietly. "I want you to know that I would feel the same if it was you and not Scotty that..."

I shrugged, feeling empty.

"I hope you believe me." Her voice was small.

My hands, deep in my sweater pockets, clenched into fists.

"Jess?" She looked terribly unhappy. Then a kind of resolution washed over her face. "What you told me — about this Augusta and Nigel Shaw. I...well...it kind of fits. Doesn't it? They lost a son, too." She picked up the journal and pictures and looked at them, carefully this time. "And you say Augusta died around the same time as her boy?"

"That's what Percy and Lettice say," I replied in a dull voice.

"And you really think I've been seeing this boy? Ian?" She glanced at me with a curious, self-mocking smile. "I knew in my heart it wasn't Scotty. I had to tell myself I was imagining everything. But now you..."

"I saw them — and heard the music, too," I said.

Mom rubbed her forehead with thin fingers. "It's unbelievable. And yet...that night — the night you came to see me, I remember you said you saw something in the hall. Augusta?"

I nodded. "Yes. Except she was — kind of — black and white — like your negatives before you develop them. I know — it sounds crazy."

Mom slowly leafed through the journal. "But Jess...Why us? Why now? Why didn't they show themselves to the Parkses — Mary and Bill?"

I'd been working things out over the last little while and I thought I had the answer. "I think it's because of Scotty," I said.

She looked at me, alarmed. "Scotty? But you said — "

"No, no," I said quickly, "what I mean is...you were in this room and missing Scotty so much that — " I shrugged " — that maybe it was like some kind of energy all around you. And Augusta's spirit, or whatever it is, picked up on your terrible sadness. So did Ian. That's what I think... and..." My voice faded.

Mom stroked the journal with her hand. "He was lying in his bed — this bed — and I — I put my hand on his cheek. He looked so sad. Ill. I wanted to soothe him. He saw me, too."

"He must have thought you were his guardian angel — maybe that's what you *are*. His guardian angel."

Mom held the little book to her chest. "Do you think so? But why is he here now? What happened to him?"

Suddenly, everything in my head stood still.

"Mom?"

"What is it, Jess?"

"You're really going to think I'm nuts — " I said.

We looked at each other, and for the first time in a long time, laughed together.

"I'm glad we're so much alike." She let out a big sigh. "So, crazy daughter of mine, tell me your crazy idea."

I opened the journal. "What's the date on the last page?"

She frowned. "It's the...sixteenth of July. Why?"

I showed her my calendar watch. "It's July sixteenth *today*. That means..."

We stared at each other. I remembered Ian's last words. Hurry tomorrow.

CHAPTER 27

I WOKE UP THE NEXT MORNING AND STRETCHED. MY FEET hit the bottom of my old sleeping bag. Where was I? The sunlight glanced off a small desktop and the varnished arms of a rocker. Then I remembered and wasn't sure whether to be disappointed or glad. I was in Mom's room. Her bed was empty, the covers thrown back. Just as I was about to unzip my bag and go looking, the door swung open and she came in carrying a tray.

She was wearing jeans and a red sweater and her hair was neatly braided. A pair of thin gold hoops gleamed in her ears. Scotty and I had given them to her the Christmas before last. Sitting down beside me, she put the tray on the floor and leaned against the side of her bed.

"Thanks for staying last night."

I nodded. "I was *sure* something would happen around midnight. Didn't you?"

She smiled. "Corny, huh? We've seen too many movies. Actually, we talked so much, we wore ourselves out by eleven-thirty or so. If something happened, it must have been an awfully quiet haunting, because I didn't wake up until about a half-hour ago." Her eyes softened. "That was the first night I've slept all the way through since ... since the accident. Thanks to you."

I shrugged, not sure what to say.

"Here. Eat. Coffee and brown toast and honey. Fresh cream and strawberries." She laughed softly. "When I told Winny we were having breakfast up here together, she almost fell over herself to get it ready."

"What — er — have you seen Dad?"

She shook her head. "No. He and Percy are getting tents fixed and buying a few new ones. Winny just took off grocery shopping, and Ben's gone riding, I think."

She put down her coffee cup. "I think I'd like to work off some of this — this nervous energy. Look. I've eaten almost two pieces of toast. You can get that motherly look off your face." Smiling, she added, "Yesterday, Winny suggested that I dig up the old garden beside the veranda. She gave me a couple of seed catalogues. I had no intention of following it up. But now ... well, it might not be a bad idea. Get it ready for next spring. Do you think I could do it?"

"Sure. I'll help."

Mom got to her feet. "I'll show you the spot. Winny says it's still got good soil, but it's all overgrown."

She pointed out the open window to a distant sunny rectangle of rough garden. "So that's what that pile of weeds is," I said. "Let's hope there are some decent gardening tools in the shed. Probably all rust and rotting handles."

"You might be right," Mom said, smiling, "but it would mean I'd — what's that?"

I stiffened. Her eyes were wide and anxious.

"Listen," she hissed. "I can hear something."

She leaned out the open window. I was so tense, I'm sure my knee joints squeaked when I edged closer to her.

She tilted her head. "A wagon? Coming up the road? No. It's stopped." She put her hand to her throat. "Has the sun dimmed? Why has the light changed? The sky's grey. Look! It's — it's raining. It can't be!"

"It's happening, Mom," I whispered harshly.

"Can you hear it, Jess? By the side of the house. Wheels turning, a harness jingling — ?"

I nodded vigorously. Silently, we moved closer together.

Mom's nails dug into my arm. She was straining forward, her eyes wide.

"Over there," she said, her voice low and frightened. "By the curve of the road. Do you see it?"

The light was that of early dusk on a drizzly afternoon. Coming towards the house was the negative of a tall woman, her skirt and waistcoat white, a small black hat on her head, a white feather fluttering out behind. Her hands and face were a glimmering dark grey. She was carrying a carpet-bag. The air seemed to shimmer, distorting the shapes around her. In the background, I could just make out a wagon and two horses turning away. They disappeared into the colours of the trees and outbuildings. But the woman remained.

"Augusta," I whispered.

She came to a halt, staring up towards the hill behind the creek.

Mom's grip tightened. "Listen!"

An echo of hoofbeats came from the direction Augusta was looking. The poplars were thinner, and I could see a flurry of movement along the rise.

"It's them. Can you see them?"

"Yes, yes, I can," Mom breathed.

Augusta dropped her bag and took a few steps forward. Then, lifting her skirts, she ran at an angle towards the creek. I could hear her feet hit the hard ground, as if I had been suddenly plunged underwater — everything seeming over-loud and yet muffled and distorted. In horrified fascination, I watched her run across the yard to the far fence. She was going to confront them.

Towards each other they came: Nigel and Ian, thundering alongside a shimmering phantom fence that ran up one side of a thin forest of poplars, and Augusta, along the front edge of the same stand of trees. They were heading straight for a collision. I held my breath.

"Ian!" Mom screamed, but her voice echoed thick and slow through the air. Her face chalk white, her mouth opening and closing, she turned to run. I grabbed her hand and held on. A dark wind slowly roared around us.

"Mom!" I cried. "We can't help them. They're too far away."

"Stop her!" Mom shouted, her voice garbled and sluggish. "We — have — to — stop — her!"

Far below us, Augusta raced towards the riders.

"Watch out! Look out!" I heard someone cry — Mom? me? — but still the angry woman ran on. I could see the rage in Augusta's movements, her arms punching the air, her heels kicking up her skirt.

The riders rounded the bend. A terrible scream of fury ripped through the air. The riders' faces, shocked and horrified, gleamed white in the rising dust. Each tried to rein in hard but Augusta's hands were already clawing at Phantom's bridle.

Nigel fought his horse and kept his seat, but Phantom's eyes rolled white with fear.

Augusta's slender figure became lost in the billows of dust. Only her black hands were visible, grappling with the horse's tangled mane. Phantom reared, one leg splaying

208

sideways, the other banging in crashing echoes against the poles of the fence. The boy shifted, first left, then right, trying to keep his balance, but one leg must have slipped out of its stirrup. He slid sideways off the horse.

"Iaan! Iaan!" Mom's and Augusta's screams mingled.

Phantom, lips back and eyes rolling, reared again, one hoof lashing out. Augusta flew through the air backwards, crumpling on the ground. Phantom's other foreleg suddenly thrust itself between the rails. With a horrible crash, his huge body sank below the curtain of dust.

Nigel leaped from his horse and threw himself upon the struggling grey. Helplessly, we watched him drag Ian's limp body from beneath the heaving horse, his bellows and the grey's frantic squeals reverberating through the heavy atmosphere.

A small plump woman came running from the house. She tried to see the boy in the man's arms but he ran past her. She looked down at the crumpled body of Augusta Shaw, took two steps towards it, then ran back to the house.

The fallen grey struggled to its feet, limped towards the fence, and vanished.

Mom and I were staring at the black and white figure on the ground when it, too, melted away.

"It's over, Mom," I whispered. "It's over."

With stricken eyes she looked at me and shook her head back and forth. "No."

She was right. The strange greyness around us remained. Gripping my hand tightly, she turned us away from the window — towards the bedroom door.

CHAPTER 28

THE DOOR WAS NO LONGER DEEP BLUE BUT A DARK glossy brown, its edges covered in tiny beads of light. It wavered like old silk before slowly opening. Nigel Shaw, carrying Ian, stumbled into the room, followed by Madeline. All three seemed so solid and real—Nigel and Ian splattered thickly with mud—yet an eerie glow surrounded them.

Nigel gently lowered Ian onto the bed, then fell on his knees, burying his face in his hands. Madeline's face was a mask of grief, her fists pushed deep into her stomach.

Ian was dead.

Suddenly Mom's fingers crushed mine. Nigel Shaw was coming towards us. Edging quickly to one side, we clung together, but of course, he didn't even see us. He stood at the window, gazing down into the yard. I could see the splashes of drying mud in his hair and a jagged tear in the shoulder of his shirt.

After saying something to Madeline—which we heard only as a faint whisper in the air—he turned and walked past us to the door. His eyes held a fixed intensity; his arms were locked across his chest, as if embracing his terrible pain.

Madeline stood beside Ian's bed, one hand clamped over her mouth, tears washing her round cheeks. Then she reached forward and gently brushed his hair off his forehead before covering his entire body with a light quilt that had been hanging on the end of the bed. Slowly, bent over with grief, she left the room, shutting the door.

"We — we have to leave," I whispered, but Mom shook her head.

It was then that I heard the faint tapping of heels coming down the hall. The bones in my body rattled when unseen fists pounded on the door. A loud keening wail was followed quickly by another. My scalp crawled with terror.

Mom's face was drawn and pale. "Wha — why can't she come in?"

My lips barely moved. "Ian won't let her."

The wailing grew louder and louder, the pounding went on and on. Dazed with misery, Mom and I huddled together.

Then Mom cried, "We can't do this! It's her son! It's not right!" She ran to the door.

Somehow, a part of my mind was surprised I hadn't stopped her, but another part knew I shouldn't. She flung the door open to the black and white figure waiting on the other side. It seemed to float into the room, the tapping of the unseen heels clear and light.

The moment it crossed the threshold, it began to change, turning into a tall woman in a deep blue dress and jacket. The once tightly coiled hair had fallen loose and the clothes were torn and covered in thick mud. Grimacing with pain, she clutched her side. Through strands of wet black hair, the pale face and dark eyes focused on the small still figure. She drew herself up and closed her eyes as if protecting —

almost exalting in—her pain. At the same time, her long fingers plucked and pulled at the dress, tearing the soiled lace.

Shock flushed through me like icy water when first the gossamer face and then the pale hands of Ian Shaw appeared, suspended in the air. Slowly, he fully emerged in the dusky light, standing alongside the body under the shroud.

He was looking at Augusta, his pale luminous face wondering and sad.

"Betrayal," a voice whispered. "Sorry...sorry..."

Ian moved slowly forward, his body passing through the corner of the bed. That's when Augusta opened her eyes and saw him. She stepped back, her tortured eyes staring. After what seemed an inner struggle, Ian held out his hand.

She shook her head back and forth, back and forth. "Betrayed," the voice whispered. "Can't...forgive... me...can't..."

She had been betrayed. She had killed her son. How could he forgive her? How could she forgive him? A great ache rose in my throat.

Gently Mom released my hand and stepped between the mother and son. Augusta saw her. She studied Mom, a frown puckering her forehead, as if trying to recognize her. Then something happened between them—an acknowledgement or understanding of some kind. Augusta's face melted into an unguarded mixture of pain and weariness and sorrow. Mom reached out.

To my amazement, Augusta allowed her hand to be taken. Then Mom turned to Ian. His face instantly lit up with joyful recognition and he took her other hand.

"Ian?" a distant voice whispered. "Ian?"

Ian looked at his mother with a sad smile, only a trace of

212

bitterness remaining. Augusta nodded. Her eyes closed peacefully, and with a sigh of great weariness, she slowly vanished. Ian gazed at Mom as if trying to memorize her face. Then, he too began to fade.

"Ian!" Mom cried out. "*No*! Ian...Scotty...oh, no..."

But Ian had released her hand. The quilt, the body, and Ian's gentle spirit were gone.

I put my arms around Mom's thin shoulders, silent with anguish. Then, she groped for my hand and we sat on the bed.

"Jeanie?"

Startled, we looked up. Dad, his long face flushed, stood at the door.

"I—I heard you—I was in the hall...and I—" His dark eyes pleaded.

Mom nodded and reached out her free hand. Hesitant, uneasy, Dad came to sit beside us. With a kind of wonder, he traced the tears on her face with one finger. "Jeanie, I—"

Mom nodded. In her eyes, for the first time, I saw a kind of peace, an inner stillness.

Just then, a sharp whistle sounded outside. Leaning out the window, I saw Ben standing in the yard below.

"So, you're finally up, huh?" he called.

He was holding Bower and a horse I didn't recognize. Both were saddled. Sun and shadow from the big poplar by the veranda dappled across them.

"I've gotta try out this new fella. Wanna come? Do you think you can risk riding Bower?"

"What risk? I'll be right there." My voice shook, but I was grinning.

He looked at me kind of funny, but I just laughed. Leaving my parents talking quietly together, I ran downstairs.

I knew this wasn't going to be a perfect ending—or a

213

perfect new beginning. But maybe we'd all take some risks now. Yeah, why not? I was sure Ian Shaw didn't regret the ones he'd taken. And I also knew that on such a beautiful day, he'd be out riding his phantom horse down that dark green valley—his face alight, loving every second of his precious freedom.

About the author

Margaret Buffie is a writer and artist living in Winnipeg, Manitoba. She has had a lifelong interest in the supernatural and was inspired to write *My Mother's Ghost* after visiting a haunted ranch. Buffie has written two other novels for young adults, *Who is Frances Rain?* and *The Guardian Circle*. She is currently at work on a mystery for adults.

Printed in Canada